Ella Matthews lives and works in beautiful South Wales. When she's not thinking about handsome heroes she can be found walking along the coast with her husband and their two children—probably still thinking about heroes, but at least pretending to be interested in everyone else…

THE KNIGHT'S BRIDE PRIZE

Ella Matthews

MILLS & BOON

First published in Great Britain 2024
by Mills & Boon, an imprint of HarperCollins*Publishers* Ltd,
1 London Bridge Street, London, SE1 9GF

www.harpercollins.co.uk

HarperCollins*Publishers*, Macken House, 39/40 Mayor Street Upper, Dublin 1, D01 C9W8, Ireland

The Knight's Bride Prize © 2024 Ella Matthews

ISBN: 978-0-263-32101-2

11/24

This book contains FSC™ certified paper and other controlled sources to ensure responsible forest management.

For more information visit www.harpercollins.co.uk/green.

Printed and Bound in the UK using 100% Renewable Electricity at CPI Group (UK) Ltd, Croydon, CR0 4YY

To Annie Grimshaw

Chapter One

Wales 1337

Hugh twisted in his saddle, glancing back to look at his travelling companion. Tristan, one of Hugh's oldest friends, was staring glumly into the treeline, his shoulders slumped and his lips downturned. His demeanour was so at odds with his normal jovial countenance that Hugh almost held back from pointing out that Tristan had given bad advice earlier, *almost*. Besides, goading his friend might get him out of his current low mood. It was worth a try. 'We should have taken that right turn.'

Tristan straightened. '*That* was not the path to the wealthiest castle in the area. It was nothing but a dirt track.'

'We're not looking for Windsor. It was exactly how the route to a castle in the backend of Wales would look.'

Tristan's eyes flashed and Hugh was glad to see the spark returning to his companion. 'I didn't know you were such an expert on a country you have never travelled to before.'

Tristan had a point. Before this expedition to Wales, Hugh had only travelled from Croxton Castle, his family's stronghold, to Lord Ormand's castle on the south coast of England, and that had been over fourteen years ago. Unlike other pages and squires, he'd not returned to his parents' home since leaving, not even for a fleeting visit. He was of no interest to his family who resided there. 'While I am not the most travelled of knights, I still say that was the correct turn. We've travelled much farther on this path than the last instructions indicated we should.'

Tristan muttered something under his breath, which Hugh decided not to ask him to repeat. Neither did he insist on heading back the way they had come. They rode in silence for a while. Somewhere to their left, hidden by tall trees, the sea rumbled. To their right, an ancient woodland creaked and groaned. It was hard to think anything other than dark thoughts, to second guess everything that had led to this point or, worse, to consider what was to come next.

They rounded another corner, and the narrow path stretched into the distance until it veered slightly to the left and disappeared from view. 'You might be right,' Tristan conceded. 'We should have reached Ceinwen before now. Do you want to turn round and find that side track?'

Now that Tristan agreed with him, Hugh wanted to prolong his arrival for as long as possible. 'This road has to lead somewhere. What say we follow it to the end and find a tavern? An ale would not go amiss.' He knew he couldn't put off the start of his mission for long, the success of his future, hell, the future of Tristan and their third friend, Leo, also hung in the balance. He *needed* to succeed and yet…to do so, he would need to lie and deceive convincingly, and anyone who knew him knew those were not skills he possessed. Give him a lance, a sword or a bow, and he would thrive, but this…

'I say, that sounds like a grand idea,' Tristan agreed, sounding relieved at Hugh's suggestion.

Hugh knew why he was putting off the start of his mission, but he wasn't sure why Tristan was also reluctant to begin. Tristan was departing for his own task as soon as they found Ceinwen Castle, but his assignment was straightforward and didn't involve entering a tournament to win a woman's hand in marriage, all the while investigating whether the lord of the castle was committing treason. Just thinking about what lay ahead for him made Hugh want to lose the meagre lunch he'd consumed earlier.

'How do you think Leo is getting on?' Tristan asked.

They'd left Leo in Abertawe a few days ago to start his own mission. All he had to do was accompany a young maiden to her betrothed's castle. 'I would imagine he has approached it with his usual enthusiasm and that he's already halfway through.'

Tristan nudged his horse forward until they were riding abreast. 'And…how are you feeling about the tournament?'

'The tournament will be fine.' That was true; it would be easy. 'And I'm sure that finding evidence that Lord Geraint is guilty will be straightforward.'

'But…?'

How well Tristan knew him that he could hear the hidden doubts in Hugh's voice. 'I am worried about the daughter. To pretend that I want to marry the lady does not sit well with me.'

'Of course it does not. You are the embodiment of the knightly code of chivalry.'

Hugh did not know how to respond to that compliment; he'd received so few in his life that it was a novelty. He knew his friends respected him as he did them, and he knew that he was a competent knight, good even, but next to his two friends, he always felt…slightly inadequate. Hugh was an excellent swordsman but Leo was better. Hugh could converse well enough but he lacked Tristan's charm. Neither of his friends ever criticised him but they didn't need to; Hugh had heard enough about his inadequacies, firstly from his family and then, later, from his liege, Lord Ormand.

Hugh knew that some of these judgements were unfair, borne perhaps from jealousy or innate unpleasantness, but that didn't mean the words hadn't left wounds, wounds which throbbed during long nights when sleep was hard to come by. It was true that Hugh held the vows he had made when he had become a knight in high regard, higher perhaps than most. It was important to him that he treat people according the code of chivalry because he knew what it was like to be on the receiving end of bad treatment, and this core belief added to his abhorrence with this mission.

'You probably won't get anywhere near the daughter,' Tristan commented. 'And if you do, remember that what you are doing is for the good of the country. She may be an innocent maiden, but her family is not.'

'True,' Hugh murmured in response, hoping the conversation would die there. It didn't matter how much Tristan reassured him, it would never sit right with Hugh to mislead a guileless woman. He knew he could not allow for this unknown woman's feelings to matter, not if he was to succeed in his mission, but that did not stop him from wishing things were different.

Tristan did not know, nor would he ever, that Hugh had once believed himself to be in love. He had thought that when Lady Ann—daughter of Lord Ormand, master of the castle in which Leo and his friends were training—had sought him out over all the other trainees, his feelings were reciprocated. He'd been proven brutally wrong when he discovered she was only using him as a ploy to get close to Tristan, his more attractive friend. When her plan had not worked, she had discarded their friendship; Hugh had obviously meant nothing to her.

The pain and embarrassment he had suffered in the wake of her rejections had been exceedingly unpleasant. The idea that he might make another person suffer because he had raised their hopes in the same way had him losing sleep. He would do everything that he could to avoid engaging with the Lord Geraint's daughter, and the moment he discovered the truth behind the unexplainable wealth at Ceinwen, he would leave and never look back.

Bronwen shouldn't have ridden so far from the safety of the castle. She hadn't been thinking when she left, taking the large bay mare she loved to ride. She hadn't thought of what might happen to her if she were to come across any men who could be lurking in hidden corners of the forest. All she had thought about was escape. Everything was at stake, her life and her future culminating in events that would take place over the next ten days. Everything had built up inside her until her skin had begun to feel too tight, as if she might burst if she stayed behind the high castle walls for a moment longer. Riding away from building expectation had seemed the only sensible option left to her.

Now, though, she wasn't entirely sure what part of the forest she was in, and she hadn't told anyone where she was going. Despite the approaching tournament, there was nobody who cared enough to ask her either. Her father was already probably too drunk to notice her disappearance, and her mother too busy hiding from his cruelty. Her brothers, her younger self's closest confidants, had long since left Ceinwen Castle. Now, it was as if she were fading into the background, present but almost unnoticeable.

Bronwen shook her head; now was not the time to become morose. Now was the time for practicality, a skill she had honed over her lifetime. She slowed Ffleur to a stop and rubbed the short hairs on the horse's neck. She knew she could get back to her father's stronghold, she only had to ride towards the rising sun, but under the thick canopy of leaves, she couldn't see it clearly enough for it to help. To keep her eye on the sun, she would need to nudge her horse out of the forest and into the open. She was unlikely to meet anyone. People did not often travel around here, because there was only Ceinwen Castle or a small fishing settlement in the vicinity, but she might. If they were unfriendly strangers, then, well, she didn't want to think about what might happen in that scenario.

Hell, even some of the men she knew would not be well met. Her father's more dubious friends might take advantage of this situation. These men seemed to have come to live at her father's castle for no other purpose than drinking and eating to excess and encouraging her father to do the same. It was a large part of why she was desperate to start a new life, so she could get away from the group of men who made living at Ceinwen so unpleasant. The other reason was to ease the loneliness that had crept up on her until it had become part of her.

She gripped her reins. There was nothing for it, if she didn't get out into the open, she might never find her way back to Ceinwen. She urged Ffleur to the edge of the treeline and waited. Above the clamour of birdsong, she could hear no sound of a band of travellers, so, taking a deep breath, she stepped out of the treeline. Ffleur tossed her head, grateful to be out in the open. Bronwen gazed at the sky and realised she was not as far from home as she had feared. The path before her would take her back to safety whichever way she travelled. To the right would take her through the small fishing village, while the left was a more direct route. She turned Ffleur to the left and pulled her to an immediate halt as her heart slammed in her ribs.

Ahead of her, two men were sat astride huge horses, those that were reserved for knights. The size of the strangers suggested that is exactly what they were. Their mouths hung open as they stared at her. Slowly, she moved her hands to her waist, feeling around for the handle of her dagger, which was strapped to her belt. She found the smooth handle and gripped it tightly, even as the knights made no move towards her. Now she was out in the open, she had the advantage of knowing the lay of the land. But she would be no match for the two men if their intentions were not honourable.

The knight nearest to her had hair like burnished gold, he smiled and dipped his head. 'May we aid you, milady?'

'I...' Fear was trickling down her spine, weakening her knees. The two men were large, far larger than any of the men at her father's castle, and their broad shoulders hinted at their latent power. There would be nothing she could do if they were hostile. She knew she should respond in some way, even if it was just to return to the woodland and move out of their sight, but her terror held her still.

The second man snorted and, muttering something under his breath, pushed to the front. 'Are you lost, milady?' he asked, his voice brisk and direct. It shouldn't have released the tension in her shoulders, but it did. His practicality, a mirror of her own normal behaviour, was unthreatening, and his calm voice snapped through her fright. Although she kept her grip on her dagger, she relaxed enough to speak.

'No,' she said, shaking her head. 'I am not off track, but I thank you for your concern.'

He moved forward again, blocking her view of the man behind completely. As he did so, the sun threw his face into sharp relief, and her breath caught in her lungs in a way that had nothing to do with fear. The stranger was not handsome as such, but there was something so striking about his features. His dark hair was cropped short, although not entirely evenly. His face was clean-shaven. Thick brows shadowed blue eyes. It was the eyes that held her gaze and had her heart racing faster.

'May we escort you somewhere?' he asked, his voice warm and gentle. 'I can assure you that we mean you no harm.'

She wet her lips with the tip of her tongue. 'I would be grateful if you would let me pass, and then I will be on my way.'

'Of course.' He twisted in his saddle, his broad body moving with ease. 'Tristan, pull to the side to allow the lady room to pass.'

She moved slowly. Even though they had been nothing but courteous, she half expected one of them to make a grab for her when she was close, but both men held still. Her senses heightened as she began to move towards them, time seemed to slow, and she was aware of her horse's every footfall, the crunch of the twigs, the way her hands trembled on her reins.

When she was level with the dark-haired man, her head seemed to turn of its own accord so that she was looking straight at him. For a long moment, they stared at each other. Later, she would question her strange behaviour, but right now, she couldn't tear her gaze away as everything centred on him.

Her horse eventually moved far enough past him that she could no longer keep looking at him unless she twisted backwards in her saddle. The urge was strong to do so, but she managed to resist and to keep moving forwards until she was past them both. She didn't spare the second man another glance. As soon as she was able, she kicked her horse into motion and rode as fast as she could towards the safety of her father's stronghold, all the while questioning what exactly had happened to her in that endless moment.

Chapter Two

'How about that one?' Delaine nudged Bronwen in the ribs, nodding towards a young knight whose long legs were swinging over the side of his horse as he made to jump down. 'I bet he's big all over.' Delaine waggled her eyebrows and Bronwen couldn't help the giggle that escaped her.

Growing up, Delaine had been Bronwen's closest female companion, but over recent years that friendship had gradually faded away. Delaine was now a wife and mother, but the distancing had begun before that change had taken place and had more to do with Bronwen than she would care to admit.

The worse her father's behaviour had become, the more Bronwen's mother had retreated into herself and the more awkward Bronwen had become around the other castle inhabitants. It was hard to know what to tell those close to her when she also had no idea what mood their lord and master would be in. Her father either made castle life miserable or he made grand over-the-top gestures, this extravagant tournament being a prime example of his more grandiose ideas. Some people would be expected to work until they dropped, others would get to drink, eat and be merry on Lord Geraint's expense, and there was no telling who her father would pick to be the ones who toiled and the ones who didn't.

When drunk, which was almost always, he could be vile and unforgiving, his wife bearing the brunt of his ill behaviour. In recent years, he had worn Bronwen's mother down with his constant criticism until she had become a shadow of the woman she had been during Bronwen's younger years. The shifting sands of her father's moods kept everyone around him as taut as a string on a lyre. No one wanted to be subject to his derision; they had seen how that had destroyed his wife. Bronwen had been left with no one to talk to as her mother faded away.

Sometimes the days stretched out long and empty before Bronwen, and she had yearned for someone to whom she could talk, someone to ease the loneliness. In her imaginings, she pictured talking and laughing with her own daughters, on whom she would shower love and attention. To do that, she needed a husband.

Today, Delaine was talking to her, but she knew the conversation would stay on the surface. The two women watched as the long-legged knight stumbled when his feet touched the ground. 'Perhaps not him after all,' continued Delaine. 'You want someone sure-footed to be your husband.'

'I'd be content with one who was steady in character, even if he flounders on his dismounts.' She wanted a husband who was the exact opposite of her father. He must be constant in his moods and, above all, not have the power to hurt her the way her father had hurt her mother with his snide remarks and cutting comments. She wanted someone reliable, someone she could respect but not love. Love only destroyed a person, as her parents' behaviour had proven.

Bronwen turned back to face the new arrivals. The tournament would take place over a week or two at the most, depending on the weather, and in that time she had to ensure she didn't bind herself to a man who was worse than her father.

While her father had decreed that the winner of the tournament would gain her hand in marriage, Bronwen had concocted her own plan. Her father would spend much time with his cronies drinking and making merry. His attention on her and the knights would wander, and in that time Bronwen would try to ensure her favourite would win. The plan was a little loose, a lot could go wrong, but she had been thinking about this moment for so long and would work as hard as she could to influence the outcome. Her future contentedness depended on it.

The clatter of hoofbeats sounded on the drawbridge, and she held her breath, only to release it when she saw a stranger emerge into the courtyard. For reasons she couldn't explain to herself, she kept expecting the man from earlier, the one she'd had the odd encounter with on the pathway, to ride into the castle walls, his commanding presence would dominate the other contestants.

The longing for him to appear so she could see him again made no sense. For years now, she had planned to enter her marriage with the very fundamental principle that the arrangement would be based on practical reasons alone. An attraction to the man she wed had the potential for falling in love, and that would be disastrous. Her mother had loved her father, and he had taken that love and destroyed the woman she had been with his careless cruelty.

It made no sense to want to get to know a man better because the striking blue of his eyes had hit her like a shot to the chest or because his voice had been as warm and as soothing as a fire on a winter's night. It didn't matter to her how a man was built or how steady he was on his feet. What mattered was his character.

The men arriving for the tournament slowed to a trickle and gradually stopped. The man from earlier didn't appear and that was for the best. She could not afford to become distracted from her plan, and that man and her reaction to him would surely be a complication she did not need.

Bronwen made to turn back into the castle. Most of the competitors had arrived by now, and she wanted to check on her mother before the welcome feast began.

'Oh my goodness,' breathed Delaine, who'd turned back to watch the gate. 'I've already found your winner. He is divine.'

Bronwen's breath slowed. The hair on her arms standing to attention. She turned in the direction Delaine was facing, somehow already aware of who she would see. There was only one man she had ever set eyes on who would inspire that sort of reverence in a woman, the man from earlier with the piercing blue eyes. And there he was, framed by the large gateway, astride his horse, which waited patiently for its next command. Her heart turned over once, the beat uncomfortable beneath her ribs as her gaze settled on him. He was bigger and more dangerous than he had seemed when she had passed him on the path. Where some of the contestants seemed like boys, he was a man.

'He is delicious,' murmured Delaine.

'You're married.' Irritation at her friend for her salacious comments cut through Bronwen. Delaine's remarks had been fine for all the other contestants, but not him. He was not an object to be discussed as if he were a pretty trinket.

'I know, but I still have eyes. That man is a cut above the rest.'

The man gazed across the open space, his shrewd look taking everything in. He stopped when he reached the point where the other men were gathered and gave a brisk nod. Swinging down from his horse, he landed gracefully, no stumbling for this knight. He gathered up the reins and strode forward, his horse following him obediently. They cut a striking pair as they moved through the courtyard. His presence was commanding, and Bronwen could not tear her gaze away from him. 'Who is he?' she whispered to herself. 'And from where has he come?'

'I have no idea.' She had spoken louder than intended and Delaine had obviously heard her. 'But I'm looking forward to finding out.'

'Delaine!'

'For you of course,' Delaine giggled and turned to the other maidens, all of whom had noticed this man's arrival. Their whispering increased, sounding like the buzz of a disturbed wasp's nest. The noise grated against Bronwen's skin, and she took a couple of steps away from the women. She did not want to appear snappish, this was meant to be a fun few days for everyone, but she also did not want to encourage people to laugh over any of the entrants. One of these men was going to be her husband, and marriage to him, whoever he may be, would change her life completely.

Her movement must have drawn the knight's attention because he turned to look directly at her. Their gazes caught and something hot cracked through the air, hitting her in the chest like a lightning bolt. She staggered slightly as she had been hit; his forehead creased, and he made to step towards her.

She turned away, returning to the group of women and laughing at something one of them said, although she had no knowledge of any of the words that had passed. When she glanced back at him out of the corner of her eye, he was no longer looking in her direction, and she let out a sigh of relief.

That shared look had not been comfortable. It had been hot and heavy and had touched something deep within her. It was the exact opposite of what she wanted in her future husband. She would wed someone pleasant, someone who she could talk to but whose company she did not crave or whose presence had no effect on her body.

Chapter Three

The barracks assigned to the knights competing in the tournament were cramped and already smelled strongly of unwashed men. It was strange to be without Tristan or Leo—the three of them were hardly ever apart—but Tristan had now left for his own mission and Hugh would have to fend for himself. Hugh found a space towards the back and set his travelling bags on the ground. An older knight, his hair greying at the temples, arranged his own belongings next to him. He caught Hugh's gaze and smiled.

'Sir John de Motram,' he said, straightening and holding out a hand for Hugh to shake.

'Sir Hugh,' he responded. 'From the de Veilleux family.'

John whistled softly. 'I hoped the rumours of you participating in this tournament were not true.'

Hugh's skin heated as he tried to think of what John might have heard about him. Did he know of the disgrace that had befallen him and his two friends? The story would not present him in the best light, even though most of it was untrue. Or perhaps John had heard something from his family.

As the third son but also seventeenth child, Hugh had always been something of a joke to his much bigger siblings. It had taken him years to realise their constant hectoring was as absurd as it was pointless. He was smaller because he was younger, not as fast because he was a child and his brothers were nearly adults, but the irritating thing was that, though it had been years since he'd last seen his family, he still wanted to prove them wrong. He wanted them to know that he was an agile swordsman, that he could outrun most people and that he was a man the family could be proud of. Perhaps when he had completed this mission successfully, they would hear his name spoken with reference.

John grinned. 'There is no need to look so stricken. I have only ever heard good things.'

'Are you sure you have the right person?' That didn't make sense either.

'Aye, you trained with Lord Ormand.'

'I trained at his castle, that's right.' Hugh was reluctant to attribute any skills he had learned to the master of the castle, who was indifferent to his trainees at best or downright vile to at worst.

'Ah, I note the distinction. He was not a hands-on trainer, I take it.'

'No, but we were fortunate that there he retained many experts to oversee those training at his castle.' It was for the best that Lord Ormand did not take an active role with his recruits. He loved to pit the young men training at his castle against one another, seeming to get joy from the infighting that occurred. Hugh was lucky he'd had Leo and Tristan; otherwise, those formative years would have been unmitigated hell.

'The bards talk of you.'

'They do?' That was incredible to Hugh. 'What do they say?'

'That you and…is it Leopold and Tristram?'

'Tristan.'

'Ah yes, that the three of you are going to be the greatest knights this kingdom has ever seen.'

Hugh couldn't have been more shocked if John had told him he could fly. 'They do?' Hugh was not being falsely modest, he knew the three of them were good at what they did. There were only so many bouts you could win before it was obvious you were doing something right, but the 'greatest'…? He allowed that word to soak into his mind before he shook his head. It was Leo and Tristan to whom that epithet could be applied; Hugh merely rode along with their success.

John's smile deepened. 'They do. And so, we are

all doomed.' He gestured to the knights filling the barracks.

'Doomed?'

'None of us will be able to compete.'

Hugh laughed. He liked this older man. In truth he was unused to being treated so courteously by another knight. The men at Lord Ormand's castle were not encouraged to make alliances, and his tight-knit bond with the two other men, coupled with Tristan and Leo's abilities, had turned most of the others against them. He was so unused to being treated kindly it was difficult to know how to respond. 'I think the tales of my prowess have been greatly exaggerated.'

'The rest of us can only hope.' Men were drifting towards the exit, chatting and laughing amongst themselves, a notable difference to the atmosphere at Lord Ormand's castle. 'I believe it is time for the evening feast. Shall we?'

As they made their way to the Great Hall, John introduced him to several other competitors. Wallace, a gangly man a few years older than Hugh was fascinated by Lord Ormand's training regime and peppered Hugh with questions.

'Why do recruits do so well under his guidance?' Wallace asked as they found somewhere to sit on the long benches provided.

'Excellence is expected.' And failure to do so re-

sulted in swift and brutal punishment. A memory
bobbed to the surface, Hugh, sticky with a fever trying to hold his sword aloft, Leo all but holding him
upright as he forced his body to keep moving through
a set of demanding drills and then the sensation of
falling, his head hitting the gravel with a jarring thud.
Tristan and Leo's voices had sounded high above
him, their hands grabbing his clothes as they tried
to get him upright again. And the resultant punishment, meted out to the three of them because Leo and
Tristan had had the nerve to show him compassion,
something of which Lord Ormand did not approve.
Hugh had been nearly delirious when he'd been made
to stand in the burning sun, no water, no food and
no comfort for a sick child. He'd been around nine
and had made sure not to fail at anything ever again.

'And Lady Ann, is she as beautiful as it is ru-
moured?'

Hugh cleared his throat. This conversation was not
bringing up happy memories for him, but he did not
want to disappoint the men, who seemed genuinely
interested in him. 'She certainly caught the attention
of many a page and squire.' And he had been one of
them but had fancied himself special when she had
appeared to single him out, wanting to talk with him
and sometimes even spend a little time alone with
him. For a young man who'd never been treated that

way before, her attention was heady. Thankfully he had discovered the truth about her motives before he had revealed his feelings to anyone. It was a pain he had kept buried, and although he no longer cared for the lady, he knew he would never allow a woman to make him feel so awful again.

A horn sounded, announcing the arrival of the lord and his family. Everyone in the hall stood and raised their glasses. A flash of blue caught his attention, and there she was, Lady Bronwen. When she'd stepped out of the woods yesterday, so far away from her home, he'd first thought her a creature of legend, such was the gleam of her golden hair in the sunlight. His heart had stopped for a moment, his lungs forgetting how to breathe, and then reality had rushed back in. Like most women, she had been unable to speak when confronted with Tristan's looks. Of course she had; all women did. Hugh didn't resent Tristan for the woman's reaction. Tristan hadn't asked to look the way he did, nor did he take advantage of it, but in that moment Hugh had wanted just a small portion of whatever it was his friend had that made him so irresistible. Anything to catch this magical creature's attention, but such hopes were futile, and so Hugh had done what he always did and pushed all his feelings to one side and brought his normal, practical side to the front.

The moment had been over quickly, and the memory of her would have faded from his mind eventually, but then he'd ridden into the courtyard only a short while later, glanced across the well-maintained area and met the same woman's gaze. His chest had constricted, and once again he'd been caught in her allure as surely as if she'd cast a spell on him. She quickly turned away from him, moving back to the group of women and immediately joining in their conversation, proving, once again, he did not have the same hold over her as she had over him. If she hadn't moved, he had no idea how long he would have stayed staring at her.

He already knew he could not trust his judgement when it came to women and even if he had been free to pursue a courtship with Lady Bronwen, if she hadn't been struck dumb by Tristan's presence and if his experience with Lady Ann hadn't put him off trusting a pretty face, he was not in the market for a wife. He had plans for his future, plans which did not support a bride, plans which involved him, Tristan and Leo becoming the most renowned band of knights who had ever lived. Fine, so those plans were more Leo's than his, but they were good ones and they provided a direction, and if sometimes he doubted that was what he truly wanted to do with his life, he reminded himself of all the times Leo and

Tristan had made him feel like they were his family when his real one had no time for him. He owed them.

He turned away from Bronwen, catching Wallace's smirk as he did so. Heat spread across his cheeks at being caught staring.

'I bet Lady Ann was not as beautiful as Lady Bronwen,' Wallace suggested. 'The winner of this competition is going to be a lucky man indeed.'

Comparing the two women did not sit well with Hugh and so he kept his mouth shut, but yes, it was true, the winner of the tournament would be blessed to have such a woman for a wife. There was something so poised about the way Lady Bronwen held herself and although he may never get close to her, it didn't stop him craving some of that tranquillity for himself.

Chapter Four

A light mist covered the ground the following morning while Hugh saddled Guardo. All around him, knights checked their lances and the integrity of their equipment. Outside tents and seating had been set up to the land to the right of the castle's walls. Bright flags fluttered in the slight breeze, and the hum of voices in the crowd reached him. Leaving Guardo in the stables, Hugh ambled around the tournament ground trying to overhear anything that was said between the gossiping masses. What he was hoping for he wasn't sure, but he would know evidence when he came across it.

Hugh walked the perimeter of the tournament ground. He wasn't worried about competing, and his normal thrill before a contest was missing. He would win easily, although he supposed he ought to at least try to look as if he was struggling a bit. The feast yesterday, put on to celebrate the start of the tournament, had been lavish, and much wine had been imbibed by everyone else apart from him. There was a distinct green colour to most of the contestants. He grinned as Wallace gagged behind the rump of his horse before straightening and looking around to check that Lady Bronwen had not noticed.

Hugh rounded the back of the stalls, hoping but not expecting to find something nefarious going on, but instead he found Lady Bronwen. His heart stopped and his body urged him to step closer to her, to get within touching distance. He forced himself to remain standing where he was a considerable distance away.

She was pacing backwards and forwards, muttering to herself and wringing her hands, her calm façade apparently abandoned. She hadn't seen him, and so he could quietly step back and leave her to… whatever it was she was doing. But there was something so captivating about seeing her, so utterly different from how she had been the previous times he had seen her that he didn't want to move away, even though he knew he should.

She whirled around and caught sight of him, freezing mid-step. Her hand fluttered to her throat before she dropped it, seeming to pull herself together. Within a few, short moments, she was as composed as he'd ever seen her.

'What are you doing here?' she asked calmly with

no hint of accusation. Her voice was just a normal woman's voice; there was nothing unusual about it. Aside from a lovely lilting Welsh accent, there was no reason why it should send a thrill racing through his chest.

He stroked his hand over the stubble he'd been unable to remove that morning. 'Trying to settle my nerves,' he lied, the mistruth settling heavy in his stomach.

'Hmm…' She tilted her head to one side, and he had the oddest sensation she was looking inside him. 'You don't strike me as a man prone to worry.'

He blinked. He was bad at lying, but he hadn't expected her to notice his untruth so quickly. He wasn't practised enough at falsehoods to have a quick follow-up. He held himself still, resisting the urge to fidget under her cool gaze. 'I don't believe you know me at all, milady.'

'You're Sir Hugh of the de Veilleux family. You trained at Lord Ormand's castle on the south coast of England, where you proved yourself well. You are the third son of your parents and are renowned for your calmness under pressure.'

His lips parted slightly. It was not often someone surprised him.

A slight smile crossed her face. 'I'm going to wed the winner of the tournament, therefore it's my duty to know the details of every man competing, wouldn't you say?'

'Yes.' He should perhaps say more, but she had startled him with her attention to detail.

'Then why do you look like you swallowed a fly?'

He laughed, the sound bursting out of him. 'You surprised me. That's quite deep knowledge about me. I would guess that quite a few people who have known me for years do not know all that. Do you know that level of information of all the suitors here?'

'Of course.'

'And you can recall the same amount of details for everyone?'

She frowned. 'Perhaps not that deep. Travelling bards have spoken of your prowess.'

This was the second time he was being told this in as many days. It still seemed fantastical to him.

'You look surprised.'

'I cannot imagine why they would.'

'I must be honest with you and say that I do not know either. I tend not to—that is to say—of an evening, I prefer to spend my evenings in quiet reflection rather than feasting.' After witnessing the evening celebrations yesterday, Hugh could well imagine why someone would want to avoid them. 'After all the knights arrived yesterday, I made it my duty to find out as much information about each one as possible.

That was what was said about you, but I know much about others too.'

'Would you mind if I put that to the test?'

'Why would you want to?'

Good question, and the answer wasn't entirely straightforward. It was partly because he was vain, and he wanted to think she was interested in him more than the other contenders, but it was also partly because finding someone who could recite facts about people could be useful for his mission. That she was Lord Geraint's daughter was not ideal, and he would be the worst kind of cur if he took advantage of an innocent woman, but he had to get this mission over quickly.

'I'm interested to see whether you are as good as I am.' She raised an eyebrow and he grinned, forgetting for a moment why he was really here. 'I know that sounds boastful, but remembering details is one of my skills.'

She nodded, her chin tilted upwards. 'Fine, I enjoy a competition. Try me.'

'Last night, I sat by a knight a few years older than me, although he looked about five years younger. He is of a slender build and...'

'Sir William Montegu. He is the oldest son from an area known as Barland. It's a small but prosperous settlement along the edge of the River Severn. He trained in Gwent.'

Hugh whistled, impressed. 'Are you like this with all knowledge, or is it restricted to men you might marry?'

She pulled a face. 'It applies to everything, but I haven't found much use for the knowledge I have built up.'

'Why is that?'

'I spend most of my time with a small group of women. We talk of commonplaces, we embroider, every day is much the same.'

A small pang went off in his chest. He couldn't imagine how restricted her life might be. To be intelligent but not be able to pit her skills against anyone. It would drive him out of his mind if he were not able to train and push his abilities. He didn't want to feel sympathy for this woman. He could not allow himself to feel compassion for her, not when he was investigating her father.

'Well, I hope that your skills are put to use this week.' It was a terrible response, and by the look on her face, she thought so too. It was time for him to leave. 'I hope you enjoy watching the tournament today, I should go and prepare.'

'Before you go, I'd like to know what happened to the man with whom you were travelling.'

A chill swept through Hugh's body, a flash of extreme disappointment. It was normal that women noticed Tristan, it shouldn't matter that she was the same as all the rest, but for some unfathomable reason, it did.

'He has an important message to deliver and needed to make haste.' The truth but not all of it. 'If that is all, I must take leave of you.'

He nodded to her, and she inclined her head coolly, once again slipping behind the mask she wore.

He only managed a few steps when she called out to him. It was disturbing how pleased his body was to turn back to her.

She was biting her lip, looking less composed than she had moments ago.

'Yes?'

'There is something I need to tell you,' she said.

His heart hammered as his mind conjured up reasons she needed to talk with. Did she know the truth behind his purpose here? Impossible. Did she feel the same pull he did when he looked at her? Unlikely given her questions about Hugh.

'What is it?' he asked when it became clear she was not going to continue.

The tip of her tongue darted out, licking her upper her lip, but she still said nothing.

He took a step closer. 'Are you well, Lady Bronwen?'

'I am not going to marry a third son.'

The punch to his stomach was unexpected; he had no intention of marrying her either, but to hear her rejection so quickly after enquiring about Tristan hurt more than it should have. 'I don't wish to upset you, Lady Bronwen, but do you have a choice? If I were to win the tournament, then I would expect your hand in marriage, in all good faith. That is why I have entered the competition, is it not?' He didn't know what was possessing him to say all this. It was good if she had no intention of marrying him because he was not going to marry her either.

'My father has allowed me to judge two of the competitions.' She gathered the hair that had fallen over one shoulder and tugged on the ends, her fidgeting the only sign that she wasn't entirely comfortable with what they were talking about. 'Those who don't fit my list won't come first and therefore won't have enough contest wins to conquer the whole tournament.'

'Interesting.' He stepped closer to her, driven by this strange need to be near her. 'And why do you not wish to marry a third-born son?'

Her grip in her hair tightened. 'It's not personal. I want to be the chatelaine of my own castle. I do not wish to answer to another woman or man.'

Now this really was interesting. Was that desire born out of want for personal riches? He wouldn't blame her if it was, she was used to a luxurious life-style. Or was it part of some plan her father had concocted to spread his influence over a wider area? Either way, Hugh needed to find out. 'Won't you be obliged to obey the man you wed? You will not be as in control as you think you might be.'

'If my husband is away a lot, then…' She lifted her shoulders almost imperceptibly.

He couldn't help the grin that spread across his face. 'You want a husband you won't have to see very much.'

She bit her lip as if stopping her own smile. 'Put like that, it doesn't seem very kind.'

He laughed, 'I can understand your point of view. Even though you hope to choose your husband…'

'I will.' She nodded decisively to emphasise her point.

'Fine, you will.' Hugh doubted she would have that much say, but that was not the point. He was not here to argue with her. 'Even though he's been chosen, you will not know him that well after only a few days. It makes sense to hope that you will be apart for much of your married life.' She nodded slowly. 'Let me see if I have this correct, the prerequisites for your future husband are that he must be a knight on campaign so that you won't see him much, and he must have inherited a castle or be about to. Do you have any others?'

'You don't seem overly upset that you are not in the running,' she commented, not answering the question.

He was surprised she had not picked up on the fact that he had been hurt by her rejection, more so than was reasonable. Perhaps he was better at pretending than he'd thought. 'Each event in the tournament has a prize. I intend to leave here a wealthier man than I arrived.' That was true. Not the whole truth but a version of it, and although it left a bitter taste on his tongue, he was able to say it without wanting the world to end. It did mean he could befriend her now and not worry that he was playing with her feelings. He would not treat her the way Lady Ann had him. Now that that barrier was no longer a problem, he could question her about her father with no worry she would take his interest as something more than it was intended. And if he'd felt a slight sting at her rejection, well that was ridiculous and something he could ignore.

'You are that confident you will win?' She was biting her lip again, fighting a smile.

'Yes.'

This time her smile spread wide, and his heart turned over at the sight of it. 'I'm looking forward to you performing then. Perhaps we should return to the correct side of the stalls so that we can watch the tournament.'

She stepped closer in order to pass, and a faint floral scent caught his attention. It twisted something inside him, rooting his feet to the ground. 'You should tell me more of your requirements in your future husband.'

'Why should I do that?'

Because he didn't want to move away from her, because he wanted to talk to her, because her hair, glinting in the morning sun looked like spun gold. 'The men will be putting on a good show for you, I'll get to see the men as they really are. I can help you filter out the bad ones.'

She paused, her head tilted slightly to one side. She reminded him of a small bird ready for flight at the first sign of danger. 'Why would you help me?'

'Would you accept the answer that I believe it's the right thing to do?' Again, it wasn't the whole truth but a palatable version of it.

'Is that truly what you think?' Her hazel eyes gazed up at him and his heart twisted oddly, he ignored it. He'd been taken in by a pair of pretty eyes before, and he would not do so again.

'Yes.' And he did believe what he had said. Reporting back to her on which of the knights might make a decent husband was the right thing to do both for the mission—because he might find out information from her that would help with his mission—and because he wouldn't wish a bad spouse on anyone. It was also the only way of getting close to her that would sit well on his conscience.

'Very well,' she said. 'I will take your offer of help with gratitude and wish you luck for the first contest.'

'I do not need luck, I will win.' He winked at her, and she burst out laughing, the sound joyous.

He was still smiling about making her laugh as he climbed onto his horse's saddle a while later.

Chapter Five

Underneath Bronwen, the hard planks of the wooden seating provided an unforgiving resting place. On her left her father laughed and joked with some of his cronies; on her right her mother sat as silent as a grave. Bronwen wasn't sure which one of her parents' behaviour pained her the most.

'Who do you think will win, Mama?' Bronwen asked, wanting to engage the person who had birthed her but who was gradually fading away before her very eyes.

'There's no need to ask her, she doesn't know anything.'

Her mother flinched at her father's harsh words but otherwise showed no sign of having heard either of them.

Without missing a beat, Lord Geraint turned back to the men at his side and began laughing over some bawdy joke, Bronwen and her mother already forgotten.

Her mother's hand fluttered; instinctively Bronwen leaned forward. 'That one,' she whispered. 'The one with the blue surcoat. He's the one who will win.' It was the most Bronwen had heard her mother speak in front of her father for many months, and so it was some time before she realised that the man her mother was talking about was Sir Hugh.

Bronwen hadn't seen him with his knight's surcoat on, but if she had to guess what colour he wore, she would have picked blue to match his eyes, and with that fanciful notion, she turned away from him and back to her mother. It was best to put Hugh out of her mind. Besides, it had been an age since she and her mother had talked about anything other than commonplaces.

When she was younger, before her brothers had left, Bronwen could remember her mother as a woman whose eyes sparkled with laughter and joy. She had adored her children and her husband, but over the years, her father had eroded her mother's spirit.

Bronwen couldn't really remember her father from her early childhood. He'd been a remote figure, one she'd been in vague awe of, but she fancied that his moods had not been as erratic as they were now. The company he now kept and his love of ale had changed him for the worse until he was a man Bronwen could not respect. Not only had he destroyed her mother's confidence with his casual cruelty, but in damaging her mother's soul, he had taken away Bronwen's closest ally, to the point that now when the opportunity to speak to her mother presented itself, she could think of nothing to say. Bronwen lapsed into silence.

A few seats below her, Delaine and some of the other women nudged each other and giggled over the raft of single men who were lined up waiting for the jousting to begin. Bronwen's heart ached with the desire to go and join them, but she knew that if she did, they would change at her approach. Most did not want to associate with Lord Geraint's daughter in case that drew attention from her erratic father. She folded her hands in her skirt. It wouldn't matter for much longer. Soon, she would be leaving here to start a new life out from under the shadow of her father, and hopefully the persistent loneliness would be over.

When the buisine horn sounded, Bronwen turned her attention back to the gathered knights. The scene had changed dramatically. Now, sixteen men, various heights and sizes, gathered at one end of the list, the long runway that they would compete along. Well, not all sixteen. Holding himself at a distance from the others was Sir Hugh. Bronwen could see exactly what her mother meant. He had the look of a man who knew exactly what he was doing. He was not fazed by the task ahead; no hint of nerves touched his features. While the other horses tossed their heads or stamped their feet impatiently, Sir Hugh's horse was as calm as its rider.

'I'm not so sure,' she said. 'I think the one with the long legs, Sir Wallace, stands a good chance.'

Her mother shook her head slightly but made no further comment, which was fair. Bronwen didn't believe her statement either.

She folded the material on her dress over a few times before straightening it out. Sir Hugh may be lovely to look at, but he did not have a castle of his own, and he would spend most of his time off on campaign. Although she wanted a husband who was not around much, he still needed to leave her somewhere while he was off, somewhere she would not be subjected to the whims of anyone else. If she married Sir Hugh, she would not have anywhere to live, she might end up back at Ceinwen Castle, and that was not a future she was willing to contemplate. Besides, Sir Hugh might be the handsomest of the men competing, but his looks worked against him.

Her mother had been, and maybe still was—it was hard to tell—infatuated with her father, which had allowed him to treat her abominably without any fear of repercussions. It had created a monster and a mouse, and both were equally painful to live with.

Even as Bronwen told herself all this, she found it hard to tear her gaze away from Sir Hugh as the proceedings began.

Out of the corner of her eye, she saw the first two knights take their positions. She forced herself to concentrate on them instead of Sir Hugh, who was still hanging back.

'Let's hope for some blood,' said one of her father's men.

Her father guffawed. 'Not too much, I don't want to pay out for a burial.'

'A broken leg then.'

And the two men laughed together.

The buisine sounded again and the two men set off, racing towards each other, lances raised. There was an almighty crash as the two men collided, but neither was unseated, and they ran to their opposite ends unscathed. They rode towards each other again and then again, until one of them was thrown from his horse. The crowd gasped as the knight flew through the air and sighed with relief as he staggered to his feet once more.

The afternoon began to pass in a blur of horses, yells of pain and roars of triumph. There were moments of boredom and exhilarating fear as men clashed and fell, and lances splintered into nothing. Her father and his companions got steadily drunker and louder as the knights were finally whittled down to four.

Bronwen shifted in her seat, trying to get closer to her mother as her father's movements became ever more exaggerated and his arms began to wave about. He wasn't a violent drunk, which was one mark in his favour, but he did not seem to be able to control his limbs as well, or else he did not care when his arm flailed and caught her in the ribs.

Of the last four, Hugh was one, Sir Wallace another, a broad-shouldered man with a curled lip, Sir Gwilliam, who reminded her of her father and whom she had already decided she would not marry, and an older knight, Sir John, who had already been married once before and whom Bronwen was seriously considering. He looked like he might be kind, and he was in need of a wife to look after his young children. That his looks stirred no interest in her was a good thing.

Predictably Hugh knocked the older knight from his horse on his first try. There was no drama to it, his opponent slid to the ground and got to his feet only moments after he'd fallen. Sir Hugh showed no sign of triumph, merely riding to the edge and turning back to see who would be his contestant for the final round.

Sir Wallace and Sir Gwilliam took their places.

'I don't like this look of this,' murmured her mother, so quietly Bronwen wondered if she had misheard at first. She glanced at her father, but he was so obnoxiously drunk now that he was not paying attention to his wife and daughter, but it was not them about whom her mother spoke. She was turned instead to where Sir Gwilliam was grinning in the direction of Sir Wallace, the look full of ill intent.

'Sir Wallace has presented himself well so far. He has been very agile, and his long legs have kept him balanced.' Even as she said this, Bronwen doubted the truth of her words. Although the spindly knight had proven himself a worthy competitor, he was half the width of Sir Gwilliam and likely half as strong.

'Sir Gwilliam is up to something,' murmured her mother. 'Do not marry that one, my dear.'

Bronwen's heart thrilled to hear her mother commenting on her future. It had been so long since she had commented on something personal. 'I will take your advice, Mama, before I wed anyone.'

A small smile played on her mother's lips before it faded away again. Like Bronwen, her mother knew that Bronwen would ultimately have little say in the man she married. Unlike Bronwen, however, her mother did not know that she had plans to make sure the right man won the overall tournament. Sir Gwilliam was not the man for Bronwen, that much was clear.

The buisine sounded again, loud and long. Sir Wallace and Sir Gwilliam charged towards each other, their horses' hooves thundering. Sir Gwilliam flicked Sir Wallace's lance, managing to unseat the thinner knight until he was hanging on to the side of his horse.

Bronwen's father roared with laughter as the knight's long legs clung on. Following the lead of their lord, the inhabitants of the castle jeered at Sir Wallace, groaning when he managed to pull himself upright.

Bronwen couldn't help but turn her gaze to Sir Hugh, telling herself that if he were amused by the spectacle, it would detract from his good looks. He wasn't smiling; his sharp gaze was boring into Sir Gwilliam.

The two knights faced each other once more and began to charge as soon as the horn was sounded. To Bronwen the next events appeared to happen in slow motion. To start, the two men were mirror images, riding towards one another at speed, their lances held aloft. At the last moment, Sir Gwilliam's lance dipped and cut into the side of Sir Wallace's horse.

The horse screamed in pain, rearing back on its hind legs. Sir Wallace struggled to hold on, but Sir Gwilliam brought his lance across and delivered a vicious swipe that spun Sir Wallace through the air.

Bronwen's father roared with delight as the knight landed with a horrifying crunch, his howl of pain cutting through the air. 'Oh, sit down, girl,' her father laughed when he saw that Bronwen was starting to rise. 'No man wants a woman fussing over him.'

Bronwen watched in horror as the thin knight lay motionless on the ground. 'But, Father, I think he is truly injured. He is our guest, and one of us should attend him.'

'Girl, we are here to have fun. Let him get up by himself. If he can't, he's not a worthy competitor.'

'I'm not worried about him competing. I'm concerned he's dead.' Bronwen didn't normally contradict her father, especially when he had been drinking, but this was important.

'Don't be absurd.' Irritation was cutting through her father's good humour.

She would have to back down soon or risk facing the full force of his wrath. An increased dependence on alcohol may make her father easier to manipulate, but it also increased his temper.

'Besides, the man is moving.'

Bronwen turned back to look. Sure enough, the

knight had rolled onto his side, curling one of his long legs up, the other was lying in a position that did not look natural.

'Sit down,' growled her father when she still didn't take her seat.

Indecision held her still. She cursed herself for being too weak to defy his order, to go against his decree and to listen to her inner conscience to go to the man and offer help, but she had lived under her father for so long and knew how mercurial his moods were.

Her gaze was still locked on Sir Wallace when she noticed Sir Hugh's approach. Her breath caught as she watched him kneel next to the stricken man. She was not close enough to hear what was being said, but presently, Hugh lifted the other knight, standing with ease, as if the long man weighed nothing. Sir Hugh strode to the far end of the list, where several of the other knights were gathered. They conferred among themselves while her father and his cronies grew restless at the delay.

Something must have been decided because Sir Hugh handed Sir Wallace over to two other men, who then carried him from the field and out of sight. Only then did Bronwen sink back onto her seat, her knees trembling.

Without missing a beat, Hugh leapt onto his own

horse and headed back into position. There was no sign on his features that he was worried about facing such a man as Sir Gwilliam. Bronwen tried putting herself in his position and failed. She could not imagine what it must be like to ride towards a man who had cheated to get his own way, who had thought nothing of hurting an animal so that it would throw its rider. She was shaking and all she had to do was watch.

Sir Hugh's face was a mask of calmness as he gazed towards Sir Gwilliam's sneering countenance. Beneath him, his dark stallion was completely still, aside for the rising and falling of its rib cage.

'Yes,' murmured her mother, 'he is a worthy candidate.'

Despite everything Bronwen had told herself about Sir Hugh and his inappropriateness for her, she couldn't help but agree with her mother.

The buisine sounded and Bronwen held her breath. As he had every time, Sir Hugh rode towards his opponent, his gaze fixed ahead. It appeared as if the lance weighed nothing in his hand, he showed no fear as he rode forward, his horse's hooves pounding. There was an almighty crash, and Sir Gwilliam spun off the back of his horse. For an endless moment the knight flew through the air, his face contorted in shock and horror, and then he hit the ground with a resounding thwack.

The stalls erupted with cheers. Her father was standing, as others also shot to their feet, shouting and hollering his approval at the precise way Sir Hugh had dealt with Sir Gwilliam.

Bronwen realised she was grinning and clapping her hands together, relishing in the swift justice meted out by Sir Hugh. He cantered slowly to the stalls, his features relaxed but not triumphant or gloating, and Bronwen's heart swelled in admiration.

Her father grabbed her arm. 'Come, we must congratulate him on his win.' He pulled her through the crowd to get to the winner, not caring who he stepped on or that her skin burned as he tugged her.

And then Hugh was before her, looking up at her in her slightly elevated position in the stands, his cool blue eyes darkening when he saw her father's tight grip on her skin, and her heart squeezed again. No one had ever expressed any sort of sympathy at the way her father was towards her, not even her mother.

Sir Hugh's gaze flicked to her eyes, and she smiled at him, hoping to convey everything she was feeling. The gratitude she had experienced in the way he had triumphed over Sir Gwilliam, the way he had helped the fallen knight, the flash of sympathy. All of that made him worthy of the win.

'Congratulations,' her father slurred to Sir Hugh. 'The way you made that knight fly through the air was the most amusing thing I have seen all day. Far better than the way that previous fellow landed, which was all awkward limbs.' He threw back his head and laughed, and Bronwen wanted to push him from the stalls to see how he enjoyed falling from a height.

Sir Hugh seemed to take the horrible comment in stride. His face was blank, it was impossible to tell what he was thinking, but Bronwen had not missed the way he had come to the other man's aid or the way he had organised someone to take care of him. Sir Hugh was a man used to being in charge; he was not someone to be underestimated.

'Your prize,' continued her father, 'is to sit at the top table tonight alongside my daughter.'

Heat burned across Bronwen's skin. This was not the agreed reward. There was to be an award of value for all the events, and that's why Sir Hugh had said he was there, to become wealthier. The knight deserved it after his actions, and sitting next to her did not count.

Sir Hugh's expression did not falter. 'That would be an honour indeed.'

'Excellent. For the rest of the day, let us drink and be merry.' The crowd erupted into cheers as servants emerged from the castle gates carrying more wine and ale.

Sir Hugh nodded to her before riding away, and Bronwen was left with the oddest sense of loss, odd because she had no idea what on earth she could be missing.

Chapter Six

By the time the feast came around, many of the castle inhabitants were too drunk to stand. Some were slumped over the tables, already dozing, others were leaning wildly to one side. Sadly, her father wasn't asleep yet; he kept leaning over her and repeatedly listing the more bloodthirsty parts of the joust that he'd enjoyed. Each time, his words were more slurred and the meaning harder to follow. The only good thing about it was that he was far gone enough that she was easily able to extract the real prize meant for the jousting winner. The one that was worth something and wasn't the dubious pleasure of sitting at the top table near an inebriated Lord Geraint. If her father questioned the fact it was gone tomorrow, she would tell him that he had given it to Hugh with words of great praise. He was drunk enough that he would believe it had happened.

Her mother had retired to her apartment some time

ago. Her father only became crueller the more he drank, and she always bore the brunt of his words. Lord Geraint was never violent, although Bronwen wasn't sure whether that was by intention or lack of control over his muscles after he'd imbibed too much. Bronwen would have loved to have had someone she could share the endless moments listening to her father ramble on, but she understood why that could not be her mother. She could no longer take her father's hateful comments, no longer pretend that his words did not hurt her to the very core of her soul.

Bronwen had remained sober all afternoon. She had walked amongst the men who had come to compete for her hand, talked to them about how they found the joust and asked where they had come from. She'd felt at least one person from her family should show themselves to be sensible, especially if one of the men was going to be her husband. But she had been one of the only people to abstain. As the afternoon had progressed, the abundance of ale available had taken its toll on all the guests she had spoken to until she had retreated to her own chamber for a short rest.

As the light had dimmed, the castle inhabitants had staggered into the Great Hall for the evening feast. Now servants, bent double under the weight of the trays they carried, lined the tables with food and more drink.

Next to her, the seat remained empty. She had not seen Sir Hugh throughout the afternoon. She had no idea where he had gone and did not want to ask for fear it showed a marked interest in him, when she was forcing herself to have none. Perhaps he'd been so disgusted by her father's behaviour that he had decided to give this evening's meal a miss, and that didn't matter. Not only would she not miss him, but it was also best he not hear her father's ramblings either.

She sipped on a rich red wine, the flavour bursting on her tongue. She could not fault her father's taste; everything at this feast was sumptuous, from the food and drink to the elaborate decorations. She might wish that he not drink so much, that his moods were more stable, but she knew that everything she ate and drank would be divine because he would expect nothing less for himself.

Endless moments passed. Nobody spoke to her. The knights who were here to compete for her hand in marriage didn't even glance in her direction; her father's cronies only wanted to speak to him or one another. There was no point in her being here, she could enjoy the comfort and silence of her chamber if she just slipped away. She pushed back against the table, about to rise, when she felt the weight of someone's gaze on her. She froze, the fine hairs on the back of her neck standing to attention. Without turning, she knew that Sir Hugh was behind her moving towards the table. The babble of voices around her faded away at the sound of his boots on the flagstones. Her breathing quickened and a fine tremor ran through her as he slipped into the seat next to her, his large body making the bench dip towards him.

She mumbled some words of greeting, unsure of what she was saying.

'Are you well, Lady Bronwen?' he asked.

'I am.'

'Then perhaps you would like me to pass you some food.' She glanced down at her trencher, realising it was empty. She had not felt like eating, but now that he was here and she was no longer alone, she was suddenly ravenous.

'I would like that,' she replied, risking a tentative smile in his direction. There was no reason to be so strange around him; they had conversed earlier and she had acted normally then.

He smiled back at her and her stomach flipped over oddly. He began to hand her bowls of finely cooked meat, waiting while she took some for herself before piling up his own trencher. His hands were steady as he held the food, and she realised that, unlike all the other guests, he was sober.

'You have not partaken in any of the celebrations this afternoon,' she commented. It was unusual for visitors not to take advantage of her father's largesse.

'If you mean the copious ale and wine on offer, then no, I have not.' He cleared his throat. 'Sir Wallace was badly injured during this afternoon's joust, and several of the other knights and I have been trying to set his leg so that the broken bones heal straight.'

'Oh.' Her hand fluttered to her throat, embarrassed that she had not noticed more men than Sir Hugh were missing and beyond humiliated that they had dealt with Sir Wallace and not someone from Ceinwen Castle. 'I had not realised it was so bad. At first it looked awful, but when he started to move, I thought all was well. I...' She trailed off. Just because she hadn't spent the afternoon drinking herself into oblivion, was she really any better than anyone else? She hadn't thought to care about someone who had been injured in front of her. Since the jousting had ended, all she had thought about was the way Hugh had moved on his horse, the way he had seemed in control even when things were going awry. He was right to think he would win every contest of the tournament; he was a cut above the rest. She would have to ensure that he did not win the competitions she was going to preside over; otherwise, she would find herself married to a man she had already ruled out.

'I am sorry to have upset you.' His voice was as rich as the red wine she was drinking.

She shook her head. 'You have not. I am disappointed in myself. I should have checked on him. He is a guest at our castle and should be treated well.'

Sir Hugh paused, food halfway to his mouth. 'If there is any possibility of him being moved to a comfortable place, where he is away from the rest of us, I think that would be more tolerable for him.'

'Consider it done.' She made to get up, but he lightly brushed her arm. It was barely a touch, featherlight, and yet it sent a shot of something powerful straight to her heart, which began to beat wildly. He was not stopping her from moving, but she could no more step away than she could fly.

'He is resting now,' Sir Hugh told her, completely unaware of the effect his light touch was having on her. 'Perhaps the move could be arranged for tomorrow.'

'Of course.' He dropped his hand, turning his attention to his food. He was completely calm, but her heart still raced.

They began to eat. Next to her, her father belched before falling face down into his food. Sir Hugh's eyes flicked to her father before looking away; nobody else gave his behaviour any attention, but Bronwen wanted to curl into a tight ball. She was used to her father, but it was shaming to her that people outside of Ceinwen Castle were now witnessing his drunken actions.

'Is he safe to be like that?' asked Hugh after a few moments of chewing in silence.

'For most people, probably not, but he seems immune to death. So...' she shrugged her shoulders, more ambivalently than she was feeling inside. Hugh spluttered out a laugh, and something inside of her really did relax; it had been so long since she had amused someone.

'That does not sound like something a particularly devoted daughter would say.'

'I would love to be a doting daughter, but he does make it very hard with his embarrassing behaviour.' She slammed her mouth shut; she'd shocked herself by how honest she was being. There was something about Hugh that drew her in and made her want to speak. Or perhaps it was just that she had someone to talk to for the first time in so long. 'Speaking of his behaviour, I have your real prize from this afternoon.' From beneath the skirts of her dress, she pulled out a small golden goblet. 'In the excitement of the afternoon, I'm afraid my father forgot to give it to you.' She was fairly sure her father had no intention of handing out the real prize after he'd settled on the idea that the winner would sit at the top table.

All thoughts on her father vanished from her mind as Sir Hugh's long fingers brushed over hers as he took the goblet from her hand. The shock of his skin on hers was hot and powerful, leaving a burning trail in its wake. She glanced at his face. His eyes had widened, his pupils blown wide. The world stilled, and then he was holding up the goblet to the candlelight as if nothing had happened. Perhaps it hadn't. She did not know men, could not really tell if he had experienced the same flash of something hot and potent as she had. Maybe…but no, he seemed unaffected now.

'This is very fine,' he said as he turned it this way and that, studying the engravings, the gems sparkling in the flickering flames. 'I appreciate you remembering to give this to me, but you are wrong.' He lifted his gaze from the trinket and looked directly at her; the blue of his eyes was so startling she almost had to look away. 'This is not the true prize.'

'No?' Her brow furrowed. She was sure this was what her father had planned to give the winner of today's joust. Even if he hadn't, how would Sir Hugh know any differently?

'No. Your father was correct when he said that the prize was sitting next to you during the feast.'

'Oh.' Heat rushed over her skin, burning her cheeks. She was glad for the dim light so that Hugh would not be able to see the redness that must be covering her face. The silence stretched and grew between them until it almost felt like it was something she could touch. 'I am glad you won earlier,' she blurted out when the tension to say something, anything to break the silence became too much.

'Even though it puts me closer to winning the tournament as a whole?' His eyes twinkled mischievously. 'Ah, but then I can't win, can I? You are going to rig the contest somehow. Are you going to tell me how?'

She grinned, her momentary embarrassment forgotten. 'What would be the fun in that?'

'I might be good at everything, and then what will you do?'

For a wild moment, she imagined herself as Hugh's bride. She could be the one who got to lie next to him, to bathe in the gaze from his blue eyes, to be the very centre of his concentration. Her heart quickened, imagining a lifetime with such a handsome man, but she pushed the thought away quickly. He could not provide her with what she needed; she had already judged him and decided he was not the man for her, no matter how he looked. In fact, his handsomeness worked against him. It would be good if she stayed consistent in her message to him.

'Oh, I promise you, you will not be good at this.'

His lips twitched and a surge of satisfaction ran through Bronwen. She wanted to be the one who made this serious knight smile and laugh. She had a feeling it didn't happen very often. She was not going to marry him, but that didn't mean they couldn't be friends. Goodness knew, she was in desperate need of someone to fill the lonely void.

'There must be something you are not good at. Do you care to tell me?' she asked teasingly.

He leaned a muscled forearm onto the table, turning his body to face her. 'I'm not very good at lying.'

'Oh.' The admission took her by surprise. It was more personal than she'd been expecting. Unfortunately, it was yet another point in his favour. Her father's drinking made him unreliable. Under the influence, he would promise things, things she had once believed would happen, things that never did when he was sober. Too many times, she had heard him say that he would put a stop to his behaviour only for him to start all over again the next evening. She often felt as if the ground were shifting beneath her feet, never sure what was real and what was not. 'If that is true, then that makes you very rare indeed.' She took a sip of wine. 'May I put it to the test?'

His forehead crinkled. 'How will you do that?'

'Tell me one thing about you that is true and one that isn't.'

His eyes crinkled at the corners, and she decided she liked this version of him, relaxed and entertained. It was different from his calm and considered look but no less alluring. 'And how will you know the difference? I could tell you anything.'

She shook her head. 'You won't do that.'

'How can you be so sure?'

'I saw you compete earlier and I saw your integrity. You will play the challenge fairly.'

His smile dimmed slightly.

'Have I offended you?'

'Not at all. I am merely shocked at how easily you have understood my character after so little an acquaintance. You are very perceptive.' She sat a little straighter, she had never received such a compliment before, and the pride flooding through her was headier than a whole glass of wine. 'I am ready for the challenge. Let me see...' His gaze flicked to the candle that burned brightly between them.

He rubbed his chin. 'When I had been a squire for some time, it was perhaps my fourteenth year of age, my oldest brother came to Lord Ormand's castle, that's where I trained, and he didn't recognise me. He didn't believe me when I told him of our connection. I hadn't seen him in seven years, perhaps he had not been expecting me to grow.' He shrugged.

She nodded, waiting for him to talk again, although she already knew that was true.

'In the same year...my father...' He shuffled in his chair, and she pressed her lips together to stop her smile. He was right; he was a bad liar. He let out a long breath. 'My father paid me a visit and he…' his gaze flicked to the candle again, and she couldn't help the giggle that burst out of her.

He turned back to her, his lips curling into a soft smile. 'I told you I was bad at lying.'

'But you had time to plan what you were going to say,' she laughed. 'You could have come up with anything.'

He shrugged. 'I had something to say, but the words wouldn't come out because I knew they weren't true. What can I say? It's a curse.'

'Some would say it's a blessing.'

'Hmm…those who say that have never tried to get away with anything.' His eyes lost focus as if he were thinking of something else. 'I remember not long after I had become a squire—so this was around the age of fourteen also—we were…'

'Who's "we"?'

'All the boys training with me at Lord Ormand's castle. There were a lot of us. I was close to two of them, Tristan and Leopold. I was very much a rule follower. Well, you have to be if you cannot lie, but the same could not be said for Tristan and Leo. Not that they are bad, don't get me wrong.' His eyes crinkled in the corner at some fond memory. 'If you are ever in a tight spot, then those two will have your back. I'd die for them and they for me.' She nodded, trying hard to imagine what it must be like to have friends like that. It must be wonderful. 'Anyway, it was our job to carry out the piss buckets in the morning.' He winced. 'I didn't mean to be crude…'

'There is no need to apologise.'

He nodded. 'Emptying those particular buckets was something we did on rotation with all the other squires, you understand. Anyway, on this occasion, we were carrying them out and, through no fault of his own, Leo slipped.'

Bronwen gasped, her hand covering her mouth as she tried not to laugh.

'I'm not sure the wife of the lord found it as funny as you, as he managed to throw it all over himself and one of her tapestries.' Hugh was fighting a grin and Bronwen's heart swelled at the sight.

'No!'

He nodded solemnly. 'I'm afraid so.'

Bronwen couldn't stop her laughter. 'What happened?'

'Leo did not want anyone to find out. Besides the humiliation of being covered in other people's…' He waved a hand around clearly trying to think of a less crude word. 'Well, you know, the lord of the castle was not a kind man, and we feared his punishments greatly.' Hugh glanced at her. 'Don't worry, this story doesn't have a happy ending, but it is not as bad as all that. We all lived to tell the tale, although Tristan and I could have happily murdered Leo.' From the twinkle in his eye, Bronwen surmised that he was joking. 'Actually, out of all of us, it was only Tristan who should not shoulder any of the blame for this incidence. This was a time when only Leo and I were at fault.'

He shook his head. 'I am getting ahead of myself. Where was I? Oh yes, the three of us worked hard, cleaning up the mess before anyone could spot it, and when we were done, Leo spent so much time in the nearby river with a bar of soap that I thought he might die of frostbite. We thought we had got away with it, and we probably would have done if it had not been for me and my inability to lie well.'

Bronwen loved this story. She could picture three young men laughing and joking and working together as a team. She had seen enough alliances form over the years she had watched pages and squires training at her father's castle. She had never been part of a group like that herself, and she longed to have that connection with someone. 'What happened next?'

'The lady of the castle noticed that the tapestry was wet and questioned all the trainees one by one. It was awful. I was a sweating, stumbling mess, and that was before I spoke. It was so obvious I was guilty of something.'

'I can't imagine you dropping your friends in it though.' She had not known him long, but of this, she was sure.

'You're right, I didn't, but... I was questioned.'

He pulled a face and she laughed at the comical expression.

'I denied knowing anything, but it was horribly obvious that I did, and she just kept going and going. I tied myself in knots trying to avoid telling her the truth but avoid telling her an outright lie. I never admitted anything, but she knew I knew something and I knew she knew.' He shuddered, and there was something incredibly adorable about seeing such a large, powerful man shivering in embarrassment.

There were so many facets to him. He was a leader, a man who showed compassion and a man whom you would want on your side, but he could also feel humility and didn't appear to be ashamed of showing embarrassment. Bronwen liked him more than she should.

'I'd rather face an army with one arm tied behind my back than go through that again,' he admitted.

'Did you crack under interrogation?'

'Never! But,' he added sheepishly, 'it was of no use. I was so obviously guilty of something that we got punished anyway. It was a whole ten months of piss bucket duty. I can't look at an empty bucket without my stomach turning.' He grinned and took a mouthful of bread.

'Were your friends very angry with you?'

'No.' He shook his head. 'They knew my weaknesses. As soon as we realised Lady Ann was going to interrogate me, they knew we were doomed and we were resigned to our fate. In fairness, Leo was the one to throw the contents of the bucket everywhere, so we were in no position to complain.' Hugh tore off another hunk of bread. 'Over the years, we have stood shoulder to shoulder on many occasions. I know they have my back as I have theirs.'

'I can't imagine having friends like that,' Bronwen said before she'd really thought about it.

She realised too late that her statement had made her sound desperately lonely, which she was, but she would have preferred other people not to know. She valued her pride. She stared at the long column of Sir Hugh's neck, rather than look into his eyes. She did not want to see pity in their blue depths. Then she had to look away from that too because she had the strangest urge to reach over and trace the curve of his square jaw with the tips of her fingers.

'I believe I have been lucky,' he said softly when it was clear she was not going to say any more. 'Those two men became like brothers to me, but I think such a bond is unusual.'

She was grateful that he hadn't lingered on her statement. She could add tactfulness to the long list of good qualities he possessed. 'That is just as well, as your own brother sounds awful. I cannot believe he did not recognise you. I haven't seen my two older brothers in years, but I would know them in a heart-beat.'

They were good men, her brothers, which was something of a miracle considering their shared father. The last she had heard, they had travelled with King Edward to Denmark, but that had been six months ago, and she had no idea whether they were still there. If she wed at the end of this week and went with her new husband to his home, she might never see them again. But she would know them even if decades passed. They were her kin.

'Ah, it's worse than not recognising me. He did not want to know me when he found out the connection.'

'But that's...' Bronwen spluttered.

'Perhaps it was the stench of piss bucket,' said Hugh, grinning and winking at her. 'It did not matter, as by then, Leo and Tristan had become my family.'

Bronwen suspected his humour was to deflect any sympathy and to stop her feeling sorry for him. It only partially worked. He had experienced the close-ness of friendships like she could not imagine, but to have his family not want to know him was terrible, and she suspected his indifference covered his pain.

The feast was coming to an end when her father suddenly lurched upwards, emitting a large snort as he awoke. Next to her, Sir Hugh made a strange noise that sounded like a mix between a laugh and a groan.

Her father blinked several times, seemingly surprised by his surroundings. He took another glug of ale and then noticed who was sitting near him. 'Excellent work today, Hubert,' he said, directing his words of praise to Hugh.

Heat rushed across Bronwen's skin, burning her face, her neck, until her whole body was aflame with embarrassment. If the world had ended right at that moment, she would have welcomed death.

'His name is Sir Hugh,' she murmured to her father.

'Speak up, girl,' her father bellowed. 'I cannot hear you when you mumble. You don't want to turn into your mother. She's barely audible, fool woman.' His lips turned downward at the mention of her mother.

Bronwen held herself still, willing herself not to flinch at her father's complaint against her. It did not matter what he thought of her, she would be out of here soon. She was grateful too for her mother's early departure. It didn't seem to matter how often her father insulted her. Her mother's eyes would always widen at his insults, her lips would tremble and tears would form. She had never stopped loving the man who now appeared to despise her very existence.

'He'd make a fine husband, that one,' continued her father, not seeming bothered that Sir Hugh could hear every word. 'His family is a good one, very wealthy, and I hear he's tipped to become one of the leading knights in the country. Yes, an alliance with him would be good, although—' his gaze swept over the hall '—there were a few men today who showed promise, so let's not be too hasty in forming an alliance.' He looked back at Hugh. 'But don't bore him, or any of them, with your conversation, whatever you do. We want to keep him onside.'

Forget her skin burning, Bronwen felt as if it were shrinking, pulling her inwards as she tried to make herself as small as possible without moving.

Typically, her father lost interest in talking to her as soon as he had embarrassed her beyond reason and turned to the man sitting on his left. The two of them began a very heated conversation on hunting, forgetting her very existence.

Bronwen couldn't bring herself to face Sir Hugh. She picked up her spoon and began moving the food around the trencher. The sooner the meal was over, the sooner she could excuse herself, and then she needn't speak to him ever again.

'Lady Bronwen,' said Sir Hugh quietly.

She nodded, her gaze fixed firmly on the food in front of her.

'Remember, only a few moments ago, you told me that my brother was awful?'

She nodded.

'He's not the worst person in my family.'

Bronwen risked a glance at Hugh; his gaze was full of kindness. It was too much. She turned back to her meal. She didn't want his sympathy, not when there was nothing he could do about her predicament.

'Why are you telling me this?'

'I'm telling you that there is no judgement from me about the way your father acted. You do not need to be embarrassed.'

Did Hugh not understand what had passed? How disrespectful her father had been and how he hadn't cared whether his words hurt or not. 'He spoke about you as if you were not in hearing distance, as if you were a prize horse we were considering.'

She felt Hugh shrug and realised how they had drifted closer together as the meal had progressed. She shifted away from him. 'The men here are competing for your hand in marriage. It is to be expected that our qualities are discussed. Anyone who thinks otherwise is a fool and is not worthy of your consideration. And, yes, he discussed it in front of me, which could have been embarrassing, but I just told a story about piss buckets, so we are equal.'

Unbelievably, she laughed. She had never been amused after one of her father's outbursts before, they were always unsettling, leaving her either upset for herself or her mother. She and Sir Hugh were not even slightly equal. A misdemeanour when he was younger did not compare to what had just happened, but it was lovely of him to try and make her feel better. For the first time in a long time, possibly ever, she had enjoyed one of her father's feasts, and it was all because of the man who sat next to her, who had talked and laughed with her and treated her as if she were worthy of companionship.

Minstrels began an upbeat song, long tables were pushed to one side, and people staggered to their feet ready to dance.

'Would you care to join them?' asked Sir Hugh nodding towards the revellers.

Normally, she would not. Dancing made her feel ungainly. She had none of the grace that other women seemed to have, and her feet simply wouldn't go in the direction she required them, but dancing would mean holding Sir Hugh's hand. It would be warm and strong and…thinking this way was dangerous. It was inviting feelings in she didn't want to experience, and because of that longing, that strange desire to touch him, dancing was the last thing she would do. She'd already ruled him out from her list of suitors and not just because he was a third son. He was too handsome, too attractive. It would be easy to fall under his spell, to give away some of herself to him. No matter how lovely he seemed this evening, she did not want that for herself.

'I shall retire,' she said, rising to her feet. 'It has been a long day, and I am sure tomorrow will be longer still.'

Was it her imagination, or did his smile drop slightly? 'Of course, I wish you a good night, milady.'

As she walked away from him, she ignored the errant thought that she had made a big mistake not taking him up on the opportunity to dance with him. It was for the best, but somehow, it did not feel good to have followed logic and reason.

Chapter Seven

It was only the second night in, and already Hugh loathed the barracks with a deep passion. Most men had drifted off to sleep ages ago, but the noises this many men made kept him awake. It was during the darkest hours that memories assailed him, none of them good. In the black of the night, he heard Leo's choked cry as he realised that his dream of leaving Lord Ormand's castle for a life at Windsor was slipping away from him through no fault of his own. He could see the whites of Lord Ormand's eyes as fury whipped through him, challenging all his rage on the three knights who, for some reason, he loathed the most.

Hugh tried to focus on his breathing, but it didn't help. Lord Ormand's words taunted him in the darkness...

'You three did this,' he'd snarled, his bony fingers

stretching towards them, shaking with the violence of his emotion.

Hugh had shaken his head, trying to get his Lord to see sense. 'No, my Lord. We would never destroy something so beautiful.' The water-damaged bible so painstakingly made over several years lay before them all, proof that someone had indeed despoiled the stunning artwork. But Ormand was in no mood to listen.

'I have put up with the three of you posturing, thinking you are better than the rest of all of us, because *I* have respect for the way things are done, but you have gone too far this time. You will be punished for this crime.'

Hugh had reached out and curled his hand around Leo's forearms, stopping his brother knight from pulling his sword free and making a terrible situation much worse. Hugh had tried again. 'My Lord, we have not had the opportunity to do this and...'

'If you value your future as knights of this kingdom, you will stop speaking.'

As irksome as it was, Hugh had stopped. Lord Ormand may be a bully, may be blaming them for something they had not done nor would ever do, but he was still their liege, and they had sworn an oath to obey him.

'You will not travel to Windsor to try for places in Sir Benedictus's King's Knights. Instead you will be sent to Wales to complete missions of my choosing.' Lord Ormand's eyes had glinted with triumph as Leo and Tristan's bodies had sunk in dismay. Hugh would not allow him the satisfaction of seeing how much this decision had impact him, but it had been an almost impossible achievement.

Hugh had his theory as to who was to blame for the damaged bible. A fellow knight, Robert, had also fallen under Lady Ann's spell, but unlike Hugh, Robert had not taken her obvious adoration of Tristan well. He had been out for Tristan and, by virtue of proximity, Leo and Hugh too, and the damaged bible and the subsequent vague framing of Tristan and his friends had all the telltale signs of Robert. But, as there was not quite enough evidence to convict Hugh and his friends, neither was their enough to pinpoint Robert.

Leo had written to Sir Benedictus straightaway, but there was nothing the leading knight of the country could do without causing an internal conflict within a country already on a war footing. The three of them may be the most promising knights of a generation, but they were not worth risking a civil disagreement for. The best he could do was offer to see them if and when they successfully completed their missions. And so, here Hugh was trying to sleep in a barrack full of strange men, knowing that the hopes and dreams of the two men he considered brothers rested on him being successful in this mission, and he had no idea how to start.

Hugh pushed himself up and stood. It was no good lying here trying to sleep. He might as well take a look around the castle grounds and see if there was anything he could find to help with his mission. His inability to sleep might as well be useful for something.

Bronwen woke to a shadowy dream of bodies moving through a grey mist in a darkened forest. Leaves were brushing against her skin as she tried to follow, but the figures were always just out of sight. Her eyes shot open, her heart pounding frantically, fluttering against her ribs like the wings of a hundred birds. She blinked, but her candles had guttered out and she couldn't see anything in the darkness. Her blankets were tangled around her legs, holding her captive. She kicked them off, but it didn't make her feel any freer. She often felt like a caged animal. Living under her father's erratic moods was restricting at best and frightening at worst, but this was different. It was as if something were sitting on her chest, making it harder to breathe. She sat up, but that still didn't relieve the feeling.

The wooden floorboards were cool under her feet as she made her way over to the window. To be able to stare outside from within the castle walls was a luxury for which she would be grateful forever. This had been her parents' room before her father had ideas of grandeur and had moved into a large suite. He'd all but forgotten about this space because it was so small; it no longer fit with the image he had of himself. It was lucky for her because it had become her haven. In an uncertain world, she liked to watch the people of the castle below as they went about their daily lives. The routine in their actions was soothing in the shifting sands of her own reality.

There was no one out there this evening. The whole castle was sleeping off the excesses of the feast no doubt or recovering from the amount of work they'd had to do to make it happen.

She rested her head on the cool glass, hoping that would soothe whatever storm was raging within her. It didn't. Over and over again, she saw Sir Hugh's face, the intensity at the way he looked at her when she passed him in the forest, the crinkling of his eyes when he smiled at dinner and the way he stuttered when he tried to tell a lie. He was a man of many facets, and she wondered what else there was to discover about him.

She sighed. She would never know. Even though he had caught her attention today, tomorrow she would get to know some of the other men who were here for the tournament. She had her list of requirements, and one of them had to measure up. It didn't matter if the man was not a perfect fit, so long as he had the most important two. Whoever her future husband was, he had to be in a position to take her far away from her father *and* he must not be someone for whom she could fall in love. She longed to be free and without ties that could hurt her.

She made to turn away from the window, but something caught her eye. Two men were moving across the courtyard as if they had come from the same place. One was staggering under the weight of too much wine and ale, the other walking slowly but confidently. There was no mistaking either man. One was her father; the other was... No, it couldn't be him. She pressed her face to the glass. The other man was undoubtedly Sir Hugh, winner of today's tournament and her companion at the feast.

She pressed a hand to her stomach, which was swooping and diving all of a sudden. Sir Hugh had acted as if he knew nothing of her father, so what business could these two have with each other? Here they were, striding, or in her father's case stumbling, across the courtyard together when everyone else was abed and there was no plausible reason for it.

Bronwen loathed the men with whom her father associated. Always fond of drink and casual cruelty, his behaviour had worsened when these men had come to live at Ceinwen Castle. He had become crueller, his words of criticism to his wife and only daughter more barbed and personal. The men only encouraged her father's worst behaviours, laughing at the jokes made at her mother's expense and encouraging her father to put on ever increasingly large and expensive feasts, and she blamed them equally for the slow destruction of her mother. Yes, her father could probably have managed to destroy her confidence by himself, but these men made the whole situation worse.

She hadn't known Sir Hugh long, had only spoken with him on two occasions, but he had seemed nothing like any of her father's associates, and she had liked him all the more for it. But men of worth no longer had anything to do with her father, and if there was something between them that Bronwen was not aware of, then there was no future in a friendship with Sir Hugh.

She shouldn't feel disappointed. Sir Hugh would be gone from her life very soon anyway, so the tears that pricked the backs of her eyes were pointless.

She watched as the two men walked beneath her window and moved out of sight. Unthinkingly she stumbled back to bed. Shivering, she pulled the covers up to her chin. Now she knew she had been right to move away from Sir Hugh when she had. As charming as he seemed, if he was mixed up in her father's business, then he was not to be trusted.

Chapter Eight

Hugh leaned over Wallace and brushed the back of his hand over the man's forehead. Wallace's skin was clammy but cooler than he had been during the long night when Hugh had feared a fever would take the lad. This morning he thought Wallace had a greater chance of survival, although he would likely never walk without a limp.

Hugh rubbed his eyes with his thumbs, trying to wake himself up, but his eyes burned beneath his touch. He'd barely slept again, what with checking on Wallace and the general noise of the men. Hell, he decided, was being desperately tired but unable to drop off because someone was snoring loud enough to make the room rattle. One day, he vowed to himself, he would have his own place to sleep, even if that place was a mud hut. It was a small dream but one he would cling to until he was able to make it happen. It wasn't as grand as Leo's plan to join the

King's Knights, but it was one that filled him with the most hope for the future.

'Think he'll make it?' asked John, peering around Hugh's shoulder to look down at Wallace. John seemed like a decent man. He might even make Lady Bronwen a good husband, although, for some reason, Hugh didn't want to think about that possibility.

'I do now.'

'You looked after him well during the night,' John commented. 'Did you know him before yesterday?'

'No. But his fate could have happened to any one of us. Gwilliam is out to win, and I don't think he cares which of us he takes down in order to do it.' Hugh had seen Gwilliam's face as he'd ridden towards Wallace, had seen it when Gwilliam had injured Wallace's horse in a bid to cheat his way to victory. While the crowd had watched Wallace as he had flown through the air, Hugh had studied Gwilliam's gleeful expression. Hugh had known then that he would do whatever it took to beat the man. Having been brought up by bullies, both at his parents' stronghold and the castle in which he had trained to be a knight, Hugh had a very low tolerance for people who picked on those they thought weaker than themselves. He would not tolerate it.

And the win had allowed him to sit at the top table. If anyone asked, which they were highly unlikely to do, as no one knew why he was really here, he would have said that his good mood had been down to having the opportunity to get close to Lord Geraint. That would have been a lie. He hadn't spoken to the man once, he hadn't really tried. He'd been too swept up in watching Lady Bronwen's eyes sparkle when he made her laugh.

He'd tried to remedy the situation later when he'd caught Lord Geraint wandering alone across the courtyard. He'd finally thought he might have made a lucky break and attempted to start up a conversation, but the man had been too drunk to say anything other than the most basic of grunts, Hugh had even been able to ascertain what Lord Geraint had been doing so late at night with nobody else around, although from his dishevelled clothes, Hugh could make a fairly reasonable guess. The whole evening had been a waste of time, as far as the mission went, and yet…he could not bring himself to regret it. To get to speak to Lady Bronwen for an entire evening had been… He shook his head. He should not do it again. Talking to her like that had been too much of a distraction from his mission.

'Aye,' said John. 'Gwilliam's a brute and he wasn't pleased you bested him yesterday.' It took Hugh a moment to remember what he and John were talking about because he was too busy remembering Bronwen's bright smile. 'Gwilliam was saying some things during that feast that would make your hair curl.' Ah yes, that was it, they were discussing the knight who was a miserable cur. 'Make sure you look out for him today.'

Hugh didn't respond to that. Gwilliam had made his displeasure obvious in the glares and snide remarks he had sent Hugh's way. Hugh wasn't worried for his own sake. He had met men like Gwilliam before. Too puffed up on their own importance, they tended to believe they would come out victorious in every way. Gwilliam was in for a sharp shock. Hugh may appear to be calm, or so he had often been told, but he was a warrior, well trained and not afraid to use his skills, especially on a man who tried to cheat his way to victory.

He did feel a mild disquiet that Gwilliam might win the tournament overall. Hugh had no intention of winning, he did not want or need a wife, but that did not mean that Lady Bronwen should be subjected to a lifetime of marriage to a cheat. Hugh would have to tread a fine line between ensuring he didn't win but that Gwilliam didn't either. All while undertaking his mission, a mission he could not afford to fail, because if he did, Leo and Tristan would not be able to fulfil their lifelong dream of joining the King's Knights. Him too, obviously. Although, he would not be as devastated as Leo, who had set his heart on it. The two men had stood by him when no one else had, and he would not, under any circumstances, let them down.

Hugh was so wrapped in his thoughts that it took him a moment to realise that the strange hush in the barracks had nothing to do with men leaving to ready themselves for the next event and everything to do with the arrival of Lady Bronwen.

He could only see her outline as she stood framed by the doorway. The sun outside cast her face into shadow, but already he would recognise her shape and the way she held herself anywhere. He knew what the hitch in his chest meant when he caught sight of her, knew that he found her attractive and that his body desired her, but his mission should have been more to the forefront of his mind than it had been.

He should have reminded himself that befriending her would help him investigate her family. He should never have told her things about his time at Lord Ormand's castle, never have evoked a feeling of intimacy between the two of them, not when he was lying to her about his reasons for being at the tournament. He should have asked clever questions to elicit information from her. Instead, he had learned that she had a hidden dimple in her left cheek that only appeared when she laughed, that drinking ale made her nose crinkle in disgust, and then when she thought he wasn't looking, she liked to gaze at his hands. He wasn't proud of how often he'd let his fingers linger near their shared trencher or the many times he'd flexed them.

Hell, this wasn't meant to be happening to him—not now, not ever again.

She stepped into the barracks and next to him. John made a strangled noise at the back of his throat.

'Breathe man,' Hugh whispered, irritated that he wasn't the only one in the room to notice how breathtakingly lovely she was.

'Can you imagine being married to her?' said John, his voice filled with awe, and even though John seemed like a friendly man, Hugh had the almost irresistible urge to knock him to the floor so that he could no longer look at Lady Bronwen. He didn't because he wasn't that sort of man, but it was worrying that he was having such impulses. She was not his. She would never be his, and he was not going to make the same mistake of falling for anyone again. He'd learned his lesson, painfully and with scars to prove it.

Other women filed in behind her as she made her way through the room, her boots clicking on the rough flagstone floor. The assembled men stood and nodded their heads to the women as they passed. Lady Bronwen held her head high, nodding slightly in return but not stopping to speak to anyone. Behind her, the other women simpered and smiled at the assembled knights, but also remained silent.

As Lady Bronwen drew close, Hugh realised he had failed to listen to his own advice and that he hadn't breathed since she had stepped over the threshold. He forced himself to take measured breaths, in and out, until she was stopping in front of him.

His heart was pounding erratically.

Why had she sought him out? Could it be that she was feeling the same strange pull towards him as he was to her?

A union between them was impossible for so many reasons, reasons he had spent the last few moments reiterating, but that did not mean he could halt the overwhelming longing sweeping through him.

When she finally stopped in front of him and lifted her gaze to his, her eyes did not hold the same warmth they had last night, and those wild thoughts were crushed.

'We have come to see Sir Wallace,' she told him, her voice cool and controlled.

Oh. His stomach dropped. Of course, Lady Bronwen hadn't come to see him, he was a fool to even think it. He was standing in front of the man with the broken leg; she had told him she would visit today.

Heat spread across his face, glad that no one had been able to read his ridiculous thoughts. There was no pull on her side, nothing about him that made him stand out. She had told him she was not considering him as a potential husband already.

Hugh stepped aside so that she could lean down and speak a few words to the injured man. Hugh could not see Lady Bronwen's face, but he could see Wallace's as she spoke to him, and it was as if the man had been presented with an angel, such was the look of reverence.

After a muttered conversation he could not hear, Lady Bronwen stood and addressed him. 'I have found a chamber for him to rest in away from all this.' She gestured to the crowded barracks where the men were resuming the tasks they had been undertaking when she arrived, although with more flashing of muscles than was strictly necessary. 'Would you be so kind as to help move him?'

'I would be honoured, Lady Bronwen. It is best that his leg is not jolted, but I am sure some of these men will help me.'

She nodded. 'We will wait for you outside.' With that, she swept out of the barracks, her women trailing after her. Gone was the friendly woman from last night and Hugh shouldn't be disappointed, but he was. He wanted to see her laugh again and, perhaps more worryingly, he wanted it to be at something he had said.

It took longer to move Wallace than he would have thought. Although the knight tried to hide it front of the women, he was in a lot of pain, and it was hard not to cause him more as they moved through the castle.

Some of Lady Bronwen's frostiness melted on the short but somehow very lengthy journey to a small chamber within the castle walls.

'It was a storeroom,' she said apologetically as they tried to come up with ways to manoeuvre Wallace's gangly body into the space without causing him any further discomfort. 'But I had it cleared out and a straw mattress put in. The blankets are clean, and a boy in the kitchen has been put under strict instructions to bring him food and drink regularly. The ladies will also drop by regularly to make sure he is well, and any of the men can come and go as they please.'

When Lady Bronwen had said she would find somewhere more comfortable for Wallace to rest, Hugh hadn't really believed that she would. His experience of gently bred ladies was admittedly limited, but Lady Ann had never put herself out for anyone and Hugh had assumed that was typical. When Lady Bronwen hadn't appeared first thing this morning, Hugh had believed she had forgotten all about Wallace and his predicament. Instead, she had been busy making arrangements for him. Hugh was slightly ashamed of his bias, but then he dismissed the thought. He was spending far too much time thinking about Lady Bronwen and his reactions to her. To make things worse, he was spending no time at all making progress with his mission.

Only Hugh and John could fit into the chamber with Wallace, and so it was them who lowered him onto the straw mattress. The other man made a keening noise that sounded like a wounded animal. Hugh winced at the noise, but there was nothing he could do to make it better for the man.

'I will fetch a poultice for the pain,' said Lady Bronwen before heading off in the direction of the kitchens.

The other men lost interest in Wallace with her disappearance and quickly wandered back to the barracks or the practice ring. The women followed them, laughing and giggling about things Hugh didn't want to think about.

When Lady Bronwen returned, it was only Hugh left with Wallace, who had fallen into a deep sleep now that he was surrounded by silence.

'Oh,' Lady Bronwen said, holding the poultice in her hands. Some of it dripped to the floor in a wet splat. 'Should we wake him so that we can put this on?'

'I think it is best to leave him sleep. He didn't get

much during the night, and I am sure he is exhausted. You could leave the poultice in reaching distance, and he can apply it himself when he wakes.'

She hesitated for a moment but seemed to conclude that Hugh spoke sense, so she lowered it to the floor near the injured man's head before stepping back. 'It is not much,' she murmured.

'It's more than most people would do. You have been very kind and thoughtful.'

She snorted and then quickly covered her mouth as the loud noise reverberated around the small chamber. 'No, it isn't,' she whispered. 'But I'm afraid I have limited resources. If this were my castle, I would ensure he was receiving the best treatment, but I'm afraid as he no longer has any entertainment value for my father, Sir Wallace has been forgotten about by everyone in my family save me.'

This was not the same Lady Bronwen that Hugh had dined with last night. That woman had been soft and full of smiles; this one was edgy and brittle. It was unfortunate for him that he didn't like her any less for it.

'Come, we should leave him rest.' He indicated that she should precede him into the corridor outside the chamber.

She nodded but didn't say anything as they began to wend their way back out of the castle towards the outside.

'Lady Bronwen,' he said when they had gone a few paces. 'Have I done something to offend you?'

'What makes you think that?' she asked. Interesting that she had not denied it.

'Because you are so different towards me than you were last night. I thought we were becoming friends, but today I get the distinct impression you are annoyed with me. As we have not seen one another since you left the feast last night, I am at a loss as to what I could have done.'

She came to an abrupt halt directly in front of him. The move was so unexpected that he slammed into her. She stumbled, and his arms came around her to catch her before she fell. Holding her was a mistake. His body reacted instantly. Now he knew that she fit against him perfectly, that her light brown hair was soft against his chin and that she smelled faintly of flowers. Now that she was in his arms, he did not want to let her go. He should, he knew that, but he couldn't make himself drop his arms. For all her frostiness, she wasn't stepping out of his hold either.

'Why were you with my father last night?'

Hugh froze. He had no idea what she was talking about.

'I saw you walking across the courtyard with him.'

'Oh, that.'

'Yes, that.' She turned in his hold and glowered up

at him. Her deep frown shouldn't have made her even more adorable, but it did.

'I don't know if you've ever slept in a barracks before—' He did know. She hadn't. He wasn't even sure why he had said it. Perhaps to provoke her. '—but it isn't the most peaceful night's sleep. I was outside trying to get some peace when I saw your father stumbling along. It didn't seem sensible to leave him, so I followed.' Luckily for him, that was all true, although all that was not said curdled in his stomach. He hated lying to her, hated that he was yet another person in her life who wasn't treating her with the respect that she deserved.

He still hadn't let Bronwen go. His mind was screaming at him, reminding him of all the reasons he should. And yet, his arms flexed, slightly tightening his grip.

'So, you didn't speak with him?'

'No, he was…' He paused searching for the kindest way to say that the man had been incapable of speech. '…not in the mood to converse.'

If Hugh hadn't been holding her, he wouldn't have been able to feel the relief coursing through her. She sagged slightly in his arms, the movement bringing her chest closer to his. Now there was only a whisper of air between them. He swallowed. It would be so easy to pull her closer, to lean down and press his lips to hers. She may never have been kissed before and he would be her first. Possessiveness swept through him, hot, heavy and powerful. He'd felt nothing like it, had never expected to feel anything like it, not for any woman but especially not this one, the daughter of the man standing between him and the achievement of his friends' dreams. He should let her go... he would let her go...in a moment.

He swallowed, trying to clear the fog of lust from his mind. He had questions he should be asking her, important ones. So it made no sense for him to be studying the thickness of her bottom lip. He should ask her something, but he was dipping his head, the urge to taste her a visceral, living thing. His instincts were drowning out the voice in his head... Her eyes widened slightly and reason slammed into him. He couldn't touch her; he couldn't even hold her. He slowly dropped his hold, his fingers trailing along the length of her arms learning the shape of her, knowing that he would not touch her in such a way again. He forced his mind back to the mission. 'Why would it be a problem for me to talk to him?'

This time, it was her turn to freeze, her skin paling.

'There is no reason,' she said eventually. Hugh waited quietly, hoping she would fill the silence. 'It's only that he is not himself when he is under the influence of ale and wine. You saw how rude he was to you over the dinner. I was worried he might have been worse.'

'Is that all?' he asked softly. He was a cur to press her for information when she was clearly unhappy, but she obviously knew something, and he was here to find out what that something was. He was not here to make Lady Bronwen comfortable, even though her downturned lips made him want to challenge Lord Geraint to a duel. He had something truly precious in his daughter, and he did not treasure her or treat her in the way she deserved. From what Hugh could see, nobody did. Despite how many men appeared to be spellbound by her looks, she appeared to be alone in a sea of people. Hugh yearned to be the one who eased that loneliness. That he knew it couldn't be him was cutting him to the core.

'Yes, that is all.' Her gaze turned to him and his heart did that telltale flip, which he was determined to ignore. 'What else could it be?'

'I don't know,' he said truthfully. 'Only that your manner towards me is very different this morning, which seems like an extreme reaction when you are worried that your father has been rude to me.'

For a long moment, their gazes held. He forced himself not to fidget under her stare. Leo and Tristan had told him, more than once, that this was how people could tell he was lying, and this time he had nothing to hide, aside from his investigation.

She dropped her gaze first. 'I... I worry that people take advantage of him when he is in an altered state.'

'Does that happen?'

'Sometimes,' she finished quietly, and a small splinter cracked his heart. Lady Bronwen may not be aware of exactly what was wrong with her father, but she did know something, and Hugh would have to make it part of his mission to find out what that was. He really did not want to use her in this way, would far rather enter a thousand battles, but he would do it because that was the right thing to do.

'What...' he began, his throat tight.

'There you are, Lady Bronwen.' One of Lady Bronwen's women stood at the end of the corridor, her eyes dancing with mischief, and he realised just how close he was standing to Bronwen. 'You are required in the stalls. The next tournament is about to begin.'

'Excellent,' said Lady Bronwen, her voice high and false. 'I wish you well in the next contest, Sir Hugh.' With that, she swept off down the corridor and away from him, and he was left with the sensation that he had somehow failed, but not for the reason he was at Ceinwen Castle.

Chapter Nine

'You and that handsome knight, hey?' Delaine nudged Bronwen's arm as they approached the stalls. 'Did you get up to anything in the corridor?'

Bronwen could still feel Sir Hugh's arms banding around her, the way he held her upright and had not let her go well past the moment when she had needed his support. She could have moved away at any moment, and yet she hadn't. Instead she'd watched the way his pulse had beat at the base of his neck, fighting the urge to lean over and press her lips to it, and there had been that moment when she had thought he was bending towards her, his gaze fixed on her mouth, and she had thought he was about to place his lips against hers. She must have been wrong about that, because he hadn't and he'd had every opportunity.

'Well?' Delaine prompted. 'Do you finally know what it's like to be kissed?'

'Delaine,' Bronwen hissed. 'Keep your voice down.'

'Why? It's not as if anyone can hear us.' That was true, but Bronwen still didn't want to start any false rumours. If any of the competing knights thought that she was free with her favours, she would be in a world of trouble. Her remonstration didn't stop Delaine, whose eyes were sparkling with amusement. 'You need to kiss a few of them before you get married. You don't want to find out your future husband doesn't know what to do with his mouth. You could end up with a slobbery one.' Delaine pulled a face. 'I can't imagine a lifetime of that. You won't have that problem with your knight, he looks like a man who knows what he is doing.'

Sensation flooded through Bronwen. She could almost feel the brush of his mouth, his strong confident hands and hear a groan meant only for her. She stumbled, her cheeks blazing.

'Oh my goodness, you did kiss him.'

'I did not!' But she could imagine it. His mouth would be firm but soft; he'd take control but he wouldn't force. He'd take his time getting to know her, and she would slip her fingers into his hair. Her heart beat quicker and there was something strange happening to her legs. Her knees were turning to liquid as images crowded her mind, each one more delicious than the last.

'You really should give him a try. I am sure that

he would be very keen on the idea. He looks at you like you're a marzipan treat and he wants to devour you in one bite.'

Bronwen fanned her face, her skin burning. 'He does not.' Even as she said it, she knew she was lying. He *had* looked at her like that, right before she had thought he would kiss her, but it had gone in a flash to be replaced with an emotion she hadn't been able to read.

Delaine tsked.

Before she could carry on, Bronwen leapt in with 'The competition will start soon and we wouldn't want to miss watching any of these knights fighting, would we?' Bronwen tried a smile that didn't come naturally but which seemed to please Delaine because she linked arms with Bronwen and began to gossip once more as the two of them made their way up the stairs to their seats.

The competition this morning was a one-on-one sword-fight. The knights were to be split into pairs, with the winners going on to fight each other until there was only one left. The excited chatter from the stalls and from the audience that had gathered around the edges of the competition ground was rising in tempo as the knights were gathered to one side. Lord Geraint's master of guards marched towards them and began waving his arms around as he explained the rules. A couple of squires handed out wooden swords, and some of the knights swung them experimentally.

Bronwen leaned forward in her seat. She could not see Sir Hugh amongst the men. She leaned farther to get a better angle, running her gaze backwards and forwards, trying to get a glimpse of his tall frame, but he was not there. Her stomach twisted even as her mind tried to reassure her that this was a good thing. If Hugh missed the bout, then he had no hope of winning the tournament outright. That had been clear in the rules, anyone forfeiting one of the competitions would not be able to win the whole thing.

She should be relieved. It meant she did not have to make any difficult decisions, because she feared that if it were up to her instincts, she would pick Hugh above all the others. If he wasn't in the running, she would not have to go against her common sense and everything she had promised herself. The emotion pressing painfully on her ribcage, though, was not relief. She rubbed her chest with the tips of her fingers, trying to ease the ache that was building up inside her at the thought that Hugh might have already decided to stop trying for her hand in marriage.

She tugged on the end of her braid. He had given no indication that he was not going to continue with the tournament, and surely he could not have become distracted in the short time she had seen him.

It should not matter either way, and yet she found that it did indeed matter very much.

'Stop fidgeting,' snapped her father, his eyes mean and red this morning, his breath stale with last night's indulgence still lingering.

Bronwen stilled, dropping her hands and folding them in her lap.

Her father grunted, but even he could not find fault with the way she was sitting right now.

The knights filed out, and Bronwen realised she was holding her breath. Hugh was still not among the contestants.

'Where's that girl?' demanded her father.

Nobody responded. Bronwen didn't know to whom he was referring, and no one else wanted to get the full force of her father's rage directed at them. The mornings after a large indulgence were often the worst.

'I asked her to bring me a damned mug of ale ages ago. Where's she got to?'

Her father was twisting around in his seat, waving his arms around. One hit her in the stomach, not hard enough to hurt but annoying nonetheless. Bronwen knew better than to complain. Drawing attention to his bad behaviour only made matters worse.

A young servant scurried out from the castle walls, clutching a tray of tankards, followed by Sir Hugh carrying a barrel of ale over one shoulder, strolling along with ease as if his burden weighed nothing.

Bronwen released a breath she hadn't realised she was still holding at the sight of him. He said something to the master of guards as he passed. The man nodded and held out a staying hand to the other knights.

The servant skittered up the steps to the stall with Sir Hugh thundering up behind him. When he reached the top, he dropped the barrel to the floor with a loud clunk. 'You must forgive Mary for being late,' he said. 'I thought you would prefer a barrel rather than a glass. It will save you from having to wait for your tankard to be refilled should you want more.'

There was an ominous silence as everyone around Bronwen waited for Lord Geraint's explosion. It never came. Instead the man cracked out a laugh. 'You're fast becoming my favourite, boy. Get back down with you before they start without you. You—' her father pointed at the servant '—pour the ales. This morning just got a lot better.'

The mood in the stalls relaxed as her father's mood turned in the face of endless ale, and laughter broke out, almost masking the first splash of ale hitting the bottom of a tankard, but Bronwen heard it because she was still turned in that direction. She was also the only person who noticed the way Sir Hugh watched her father. His gaze was cool and assessing. There was something about his stance, something Bronwen couldn't put her finger on, but it spoke of something more than an interest in getting on Lord Geraint's good side in order to win her hand in marriage. Hugh had denied knowing her father, and yet there was something there, something she should ask about.

And then Hugh's gaze shot to her and she forgot all about her father. She was back in the corridor again, his strong hands on her back, his breath intermingling with hers, but this time there were no interruptions, and he was leaning his head towards hers and...

Sir Hugh turned on his heel and took the steps two at a time, snapping Bronwen out of her daze. She turned slightly and caught Delaine looking at her, a mischievous glint in her eyes. Before she could stop herself, Bronwen grinned back and wiggled her eyebrows. Delaine gasped before erupting into giggles, and Bronwen laughed softly too as she turned back to watch the men perform. Whatever happened in the next few days, it felt good to make someone else laugh. It cut through her loneliness and reminded her of happier times when her mother smiled and her father was not constantly drunk, a feeling she hoped to one day get back.

Whenever Bronwen had pictured the tournament, and it had been nearly six months in the planning, so Bronwen had had a long time to think about it, she had always imagined that this event would be her favourite to watch. She'd never admit it to anyone, but jousting made her worry about the horses getting hurt. The hunt would happen away from the castle, so it would not be easy to view, and the melee planned for the last day would probably be more fun to be a part of than to watch. This event allowed her to look at the men individually, to assess their skills as they pitted themselves against their opponent.

It was nowhere near as exciting as she had hoped. It was soon obvious that some of the men were hopeless fighters. How they had become fully fledged knights was a mystery. The first round was over quickly and the defeated knights gathered at the edges to watch. Bronwen was unsurprised to see Sir Hugh had made it through to the next round. Unfortunately, so had Sir Gwilliam, but Bronwen didn't know if he had cheated again. She had been too busy watching Sir Hugh against his opponent to notice either way.

The next round started quickly. This time the men were more evenly matched, although Sir Hugh still managed to finish with ease. From her vantage spot, Bronwen could see that he wasn't even breathing heavily after his fight with the second man. She tore her gaze away. She was supposed to be looking at all the contestants, and she really did try to assess their abilities. As the fights continued on, she lost the battle with herself, and it was not long before her gaze sought out Sir Hugh once more.

She jolted when she found him because he was staring right back at her. He nodded to her as if it was completely natural for them to be staring at one another across the fighting ground. She looked away only to turn back immediately. His lips curved in a gentle smile and he nodded again. Irritated at being caught looking, she turned away, only to fight a smile of her own.

And then, incredibly quickly, or so it seemed to Bronwen, there were only two men left: Sir Hugh and Sir Gwilliam. Sir Gwilliam still had that contemptuous sneer across his face, the one that made Bronwen's stomach turn over. She may be arguing with herself over the merits of Sir Hugh, but she knew without a shadow of doubt that she could not marry Sir Gwilliam. During the joust, he had deliberately hurt an animal to win. He hadn't cared how much he had hurt his opponent, seeming to laugh as the man had lain as if dead. Bronwen wanted to feel nothing for her husband other than respect. She could never bind herself to someone who thought nothing of being cruel.

Hell, if her father gave the winner the same privilege as last night, to sit at the top table during the feast, Bronwen didn't think she could spend an evening next to such a vile man while trying to eat her dinner, let alone marry him.

Sir Hugh had to win this round. Even though it put him closer to winning the tournament as a whole, at least she would have someone to talk to during the celebratory feast.

Sir Hugh stepped towards Sir Gwilliam, his face expressionless.

'I wouldn't mind either of those two for a son-in-law,' said her father, a waft of ale hitting her at the same time as his words. 'Sir Gwilliam has the edge for family connections, but Sir Hugh is tipped to do well and would be a good ally to have on our side.'

'Are we on a side?' asked Bronwen, not taking her eyes off the two men who were circling each other waiting for the first move.

'Yes. We are always on our own side.'

Sir Gwilliam made a swipe towards Sir Hugh's side. He countered it easily. 'But we are on King Edward's side, aren't we?' Her stomach swirled uneasily as she waited for his answer.

'You are a naive young girl. We are loyal only to our family.'

'But—'

'It is the same for every noble in the land. We swear loyalty to our king, but we are all looking out for ourselves. Do not think for one moment that King Edward would not take us down if we stood in the way of something he wanted.' This was dangerous talk.

Bronwen took her gaze off the fighting men to check whether any of her father's cronies were listening to their conversation. If any one of them thought her father was a traitor, she believed they would think nothing of betraying him.

A collective gasp went up from the spectators, and Bronwen whirled round to see what had happened. Sir Hugh was staggering and the supercilious grin on Sir Gwilliam's face was growing.

'What?' muttered Bronwen as Sir Gwilliam pressed his advantage.

'Sir Gwilliam hit Sir Hugh on the arm,' said her mother. Bronwen had been so wrapped up in events and in talking to her father that she had forgotten her mother's presence.

'Is he hurt?' she asked, her heart beginning to pound painfully as Sir Hugh appeared to be on his back foot, blocking Sir Gwilliam as he rained down blows.

People were getting to their feet, shouting and jeering for their favourite to win.

Without thinking, Bronwen leapt up. 'Come on, Sir Hugh! Hit him back.'

Surely, it was a coincidence that Sir Hugh managed to get a swipe back at Sir Gwilliam the moment the words left her lips. He could not possibly have heard her over all the other shouting, but the momentum of the fight changed, and it was Sir Gwilliam who was backing away from Sir Hugh, the smug smile gone from his face as he blocked blow after blow.

Bronwen was shouting and cheering, bouncing on the tips of her toes as Sir Hugh's body twisted and turned, the powerful muscles making strike after strike. Sir Gwilliam was fighting for his life; his face was now a mask of terror. Bronwen clapped her hands in delight as Sir Hugh flicked his wrist and Sir Gwilliam's sword flew from his grip, landing a fair distance from the fighting pair.

The crowd erupted into cheers as Sir Hugh held his sword into the air as a sign of victory. He turned to the stalls, grinning as his gaze met hers, and she waved, forgetting in the heat of the moment that this man was not for her. He laughed, and in that moment, Sir Gwilliam took advantage of his distraction.

The crowd gasped as Sir Gwilliam came at Sir Hugh, this time with his fists. He managed one strike to the other man's chest before Sir Hugh pivoted, grabbing and twisting Sir Gwilliam's arms and bringing him to his knees. Red-faced, Sir Gwilliam tried to struggle to his feet, but Sir Hugh held him down, saying things the crowd could not hear over its own jeering.

Next to her, her father roared with delight. 'This is getting better and better,' he crowed. 'There's nothing like a fight to get a man's blood up. Yes, either of those men would make a fine husband for you.'

'But Sir Gwilliam is a cheat.'

Her father threw his head back and laughed. 'All the more reason to like him. Now let's get this feast started.'

'It's barely midday.' Bronwen was still full from last night and was not in the mood to sit at a table and eat and drink. She wanted to run or to ride; it didn't matter so long as she got to move. She had to burn off the energy that was coursing through her.

But her father wasn't listening. He was calling for the tables to be brought outside so that the festivities could continue. It didn't matter to him that the kitchen probably wasn't ready to produce a meal for so many people. All he did care about was that he could carry on enjoying himself.

Chapter Ten

Hugh hadn't meant to win that bout. He'd meant to throw the match before he reached the final two. As much as it would have pained him to lose to a man like Gwilliam, who was fast becoming his least favourite person in the castle—and with Lord Geraint to contend with, that was an impressive feat for the man—Hugh would have done it. He knew he couldn't wed Lady Bronwen. He was probably going to destroy her family over the next week, and even though it was becoming clear that she did not care for her father, he doubted she would like Hugh for revealing just how low the bastard had sunk.

Besides, he knew what was happening to him. He was falling in lust with her. He'd been here before, mistaken his feelings for love and found that he was a fool for doing so. He would put himself in a position where a woman could hurt him again.

So, no, he had not intended to win that bout. Reaching the final match had been too easy. The men he was competing against had not been trained for battle in the way he had, and their skills were no match for his. Even Gwilliam, whom he had to admit was better than the rest, was nowhere near as good as he was. But Hugh had still been preparing to lose to him. He had allowed Gwilliam to strike him on the arm and had pretended the blow had been far harder than in reality. He'd even staggered about a bit to try and make it look realistic, and he would have carried on but for one thing.

From the stands, he had heard Lady Bronwen cheering for him, and all reason had left his brain. All he had wanted to do was to make her proud of him, and so he had attacked, and the more he had fought, the louder her cheering had become. The joy of winning, of seeing his smug opponent reduced to a quivering wreck had been a thrill, but not as good as hearing Lady Bronwen shouting his name. The sound of his name on her lips had flooded his veins with something powerful, something that had made him push harder than ever. It could have led to disaster. He'd made the foolish error of looking at her rather than keeping his gaze on his opponent, but his senses had been so focused, so alert, that he'd had no problem in stopping Gwilliam's fists before they had connected with him.

He'd enjoyed himself, truly loved pitting his strength and skills against the other knights. He hadn't experienced a rush like that in an age. It had almost been enough to make him forget his plans for the future, but not quite. He was wise enough to know that performing well in front of someone with whom he was developing an infatuation should not replace the hopes of the friends who had stood by him for years.

Keeping all that in mind, he should have made his excuses and not sat at the top table or at least not next to Lady Bronwen. He could argue, once again, that it was good for the mission to be close to Lord Geraint, but he hated liars, and he was not going tell untruths to himself. He wanted to be next to Lady Bronwen. He wanted to talk to her and make her laugh, and he wanted to hear her say his name again, this time softly and just to him.

Her flowery scent was flooding his senses and making him think of things that were definitely not mission-related. He tried to focus on her father, who was once again presiding over the feast, but the man was not saying anything incriminating. Indeed, his conversation was so dull, centred as it was on hunting and his own prowess at it, that it was difficult for anyone to follow along, including the man's hangers-on who usually appeared to listen to every word. Besides, Hugh's attention was focused on Bronwen.

'Are you not hungry?' he asked as she pushed chunks of well-cooked meat around her trencher. Whatever else the man was up to, Lord Geraint provided good food.

'I feel as if I only ate a few moments ago,' Bronwen said, leaning back and abandoning all pretence of eating her meal. 'Here,' she nudged her food towards him, 'you must be hungry after your bout this morning.'

He nodded. He was ravenous. He picked up a chicken leg from her trencher and began to devour it as if he had not had food in weeks rather than a man who had just finished his own large meal.

'The way you fought back this morning was incredible,' she said and the awe in her voice had him puffing out his chest.

'Ah, that was nothing,' he said after he swallowed a mouthful, his cheeks warming as he heard the bravado in his own voice. Who was this man who suddenly craved a woman's praise or, indeed, any praise? He hadn't even been like this around Lady Ann, with whom he had imagined himself in love, and he was so used to not receiving accolades for his abilities that he never looked for them.

'Don't be modest. From my vantage point, I could

see the fear in Sir Gwilliam's eyes. It must have felt good after what he did to Sir Wallace yesterday.'

'Yes, it did feel good,' he admitted. All the slaps on the back he had received from the other knights had also been rewarding. Growing up, it had only been Leo and Tristan who had been his friends. The other squires training at the same castle had turned against the three of them, partly because of the way Lord Ormand played his recruits against one another and partly through jealousy at the way Leo, Tristan and Hugh seemed to complete tasks with ease. To have made comrades with this group of men was a new experience, and Hugh was relishing it far more than he would have thought possible.

'I was impressed,' Lady Bronwen admitted. Hugh did not like the way his heart expanded at the compliment. He really should turn and talk to the person on the other side, but in the same way Lord Geraint craved ale, it appeared Hugh longed for Bronwen's words of praise. 'I have never seen anyone fight like that.'

Hugh pressed his hand to his chest, worried that his heart might burst if it got any bigger. He needed to stop this before he became too puffed up for his own good. 'I trained hard as a squire. It has stood me in good stead, but I am not the best I have ever met. That falls to my friend Leo.'

'I cannot believe that. There is surely no one better than you.'

No one had ever compared his sword skills favourably to Leo before, and even though Leo was not here to dispute the truth of her statement, it was exhilarating.

'But I must ask you to stop.'

'Huh?' His heart stopped. Surely he could not have heard her correctly.

'Yes. You are putting yourself as the front-runner in this tournament and I am not going to marry you, so I would be grateful if you would—' her fingers fluttered against the stem of her goblet '—not carry on in this vein.'

Hugh pressed his lips together. He knew they were not going to marry, but her words had cut his good mood as surely as if she had stabbed it with a sword. 'Remind me of why that is again.' He knew why, and he also knew he should not be pushing this, but his pride was damaged.

'You're too handsome.' She clapped a hand over her mouth as his mood soared once more. Just as he had never been compared favourably to Leo in a sword fight, nobody had ever described him as good-looking, not when Tristan was around.

'You think I look well?' His voice was gravelly, husky almost, as his body tightened. It was one thing for him to feel desire for her but quite another to know for sure that it was reciprocated.

She rolled her eyes. 'You know you do.'

'I don't.'

He'd promised himself he was not going to mention Tristan. He'd seen Lady Bronwen's reaction to him when they had met on the path just before he and Tristan had parted ways. Like every woman who laid eyes on Tristan, she had been rendered speechless by the sight. It had irritated him at the time. A goddess of a woman, the most beautiful he'd ever seen had appeared out of the treeline, and of course she had been struck dumb by Tristan. Her reaction to Tristan bothered Hugh even more now that he knew Lady Bronwen knew he wanted her admiration for himself.

He should leave this conversation where it was. He didn't want to point out how unfavourable he looked in comparison to Tristan, but for some reason, he couldn't. 'You saw my friend that day in the wood. Leo and I grew up in his shadow. Next to him, no one would call me handsome. He is often told he looks like a fallen angel.'

She wrinkled her nose. 'Does he? I can't remember what he looked like.'

A dart of joy pinged around his heart. 'You were not able to speak to him.' Hugh wasn't sure why he was labouring this point. A wise man would stop while he was ahead, but Hugh's wisdom appeared to have deserted him. 'That's a common occurrence around Tristan.'

'I'd come across two men on a path I thought was empty. What you saw was terror, not because your friend was so beautiful I couldn't get my words out.' She laughed, and something that felt suspiciously like hope unfurled in his chest. 'Goodness me, imagine being plagued by people unable to speak in your presence. It must be a very silent world for him.'

'Tristan doesn't care for his looks,' Hugh agreed, relief at her words making him almost light-headed.

'No, I can imagine.' Still chuckling, she reached across and plucked a square of perfectly cooked steak from the trencher between them. She popped it into her mouth and then licked her fingers clean. Hugh watched entranced before shaking his head. Enough of this vanity, he needed to get back on track. He was here and she was willing to talk to him. He had to stop thinking about how she thought he looked and concentrate on more pressing matters.

'Who is that?' He nodded to a man at the far end of the table who didn't appear to do a great deal but who was always around, watching the festivities but not joining in.

'That is my father's right-hand man, Ioan ap Cadfael,' said Lady Bronwen, taking another segment of steak and distracting him by repeating her finger licking.

'I've never seen him do anything,' he ground out, trying his best to stay on task as his body reacted to her.

'I am not even sure he is alive and not a malevolent ghost.'

Hugh laughed. It was an accurate description of the pale man. 'You don't like him then?'

Bronwen paused, seeming to debate whether to say something. 'No.' She hesitated again. 'You know I told you I was worried about my father being taken advantage of when he has had too much ale?'

'Yes.'

'I fear that Ioan is the type of person to do this. Since Ioan came to Ceinwen, my father's...' She paused, waving her hand around as if searching for the right words. 'Since Ioan's arrival, my father's excesses have become even more exaggerated.'

Bronwen sighed, and Hugh fought the urge to leap across the table and drag Ioan over so that he could apologise to Bronwen for ever making her feel sad.

'It is probably unfair to blame someone else for my father's behaviour,' she continued, unaware of Hugh's sudden violent thoughts. 'He is a grown man who can make his own choices about what he does, but once

Ioan and some other men arrived on the scene, things have gone steadily downhill.'

This was good, this was what he was after: more information on Lord Geraint. It shouldn't feel like he was wading through something slimy as he asked the questions. 'Why is your father not easy to live with?'

Her shoulders hunched and Hugh wanted to stop, to say something that would make her laugh or to feed her steak, but he knew that he couldn't. They were finally talking about something mission-relevant, and he would have to follow it to the end, even if it felt unpleasant to do so.

'You'll have noticed my mother is not around very much,' said Lady Bronwen.

Hugh had noticed but hadn't thought much about it. The woman was so quiet as to almost be non-existent.

'She didn't always used to be like that. When I was younger, she was always laughing and singing, but gradually I have watched her go from a happy, vibrant woman to a shell. The problem is that my mother loves and really, truly adores my father, so his constant stream of criticisms and put-downs have slowly destroyed the woman she was. It's why I cannot marry a handsome man, even if you did possess your own castle.'

Hugh wasn't sure he understood her logic; a man's behaviour didn't correlate to the way he looked.

She glanced at his face. Whatever she saw there prompted her to add, 'I can never allow a man to have as much power over me as my father has over my mother. I can never love anyone because I cannot allow them to destroy me in the same way. I will never become a shadow of myself.'

The conversation had got off topic. Hugh should bring it back to Ioan ap Cadfael but he couldn't bring himself to do it.

'I understand what it is like to live in the shadows,' he told her instead. 'It would be a tragedy if that happened to you.'

This was dangerous, sitting next to Sir Hugh and talking to him like this. Bronwen was confiding in him more than she had anyone else. He was becoming her friend, but it was more than that. Their closeness was making Bronwen feel things she shouldn't, making her hope for a future that couldn't happen. And yet, her good sense was slipping away as she watched his long, tapered fingers tap the stem of his goblet. She wanted to feel those on her, to know what his touch felt like against her skin. She should return to her planned conversation, the one where she asked him not to win any more competitions, but she found she couldn't.

She took a sip of her wine. It was rich and heavy

and did nothing to dispel her growing awareness of the man sitting next to her.

Servants were rushing around the long tables, bringing more wine and trays covered in marzipan treats. Men and women were laughing and leaving the tables, sometimes in groups but more often in pairs, and the knowledge of what they might get up to was not helping.

The midday sun was beating down on them, making her even thirstier, but the more she drank the more the afternoon began to take on a hazy sheen, as if it were all part of some dream.

'Have any of the other knights taken your fancy?' Sir Hugh said, nodding his head to the long table around which most of the knights were seated.

As they watched, one of them slid off the bench, his back hitting the floor, his legs in the air. The men around him roared with laughter and pulled him back up.

'Not him, perhaps,' said Hugh, his lips twitching. 'You want someone who manages to sit upright after an ale or two.'

'But not one who drinks to excess,' she added, because that was also important. She noticed that Hugh did not indulge much, but that should not endear him even further to her.

'He is out then. Let's see. John seems like a pleasant enough man. He helped me with Wallace during the night, and he thinks you are beautiful.'

She stiffened. It shouldn't bother her that Hugh was offering to help her weed out the potential husbands in the group of men, but it did.

'I wouldn't recommend Gwilliam. He has a nasty streak a mile wide. He would not be a comfortable man to live with.'

'My father seems to like him,' she said, although why she said it, she wasn't sure. Perhaps it was to needle Hugh, because she had no intention of marrying Sir Gwilliam. Not for all the money in the kingdom would she tie herself to a man who would cheat at jousting and try to hit a man when his back was turned. He was worse than her father, and that was a hard mark to earn.

'If your father allows you to marry him, then he is a fool,' Hugh growled.

Bronwen shrugged, trying to tamp down how pleased she was by Hugh's irritation. 'My father thinks he has a say in this, and I'm going to give every appearance of going along with what he decides, but I plan to be the one in charge of the decision.'

'Your father seems to be a man with strong opinions. I cannot imagine him letting you decide with whom he will make this alliance, because isn't that what this marriage is all about, forming a good relationship with a powerful family?'

'Maybe for my father, but not for me. Besides, I do not think any of the men gathered here are from a bad family, present company excluded.'

He reared back as if struck. 'My family has impeccable lineage.'

'I know that, but they can hardly be good if they do not recognise one of their own when faced with them,' she said, reminding him of what he had told her last night. 'They cannot be good people if they do not want to know you, can they?' She wasn't sure why she was so irritated with Sir Hugh when he was doing exactly what he had promised he would do.

Some rigidity left his body. 'I suppose,' he agreed.

He turned his gaze back to the assembled knights. 'Aethon might be a good match. He proved himself well today, only losing out to Gwilliam because the damned coward cheated again. Aethon is pleasant and—hey, where are you going?'

'I am finding this heat too much, if you will excuse me.' She strode away from the table, heading back into the castle, knowing the burning pain in her chest was ridiculous. She had told Sir Hugh she was not going to marry him, had listed the reasons, and now she was storming off because he was sitting there, calmly discussing her other options for husbands. She shouldn't have wanted to stab him with her spoon, but it had somehow taken all of her willpower to slip the utensil back into its pouch and rise from the table with dignity.

She stood in the shade afforded by the high castle walls and breathed slowly in and out. It was a technique she'd found had helped her when dealing with her father. That she had to use it after speaking to Sir Hugh was yet another sign that he was entirely unsuitable for her.

Once her heart rate returned to normal, she set off towards the inner castle. She would check on Sir Wallace and ensure that the wounded man was comfortable, and then she would visit with her mother. Perhaps, when the tables had all been put away and the castle and its inhabitants had gone on their way, she would take a cooling walk down to the river. Maybe she would even bathe.

She stepped out of the shadow and right into Sir Hugh's chest. 'What?' she said into his shirt. 'Where...?' But standing so close to him robbed her of her ability to form a complete question.

'That's the second time I have had to hold you up today,' he commented, reminding her that she was cross with him.

'I wouldn't have crashed into you if you hadn't sneaked up on me,' she said, disentangling herself.

'Then I apologise for my body being in your way and for causing your head to collide with my chest.'

'Oh,' she said. 'Did I hurt you?'

He smiled. 'No. I was only trying to make you feel bad after you abandoned me at the table. The man on the other side of me wanted to talk to me about slugs.' He pulled a face and she giggled.

'In what way?'

'They are a blight on trying to grow food apparently. I made my excuses before I could find out any more. You are welcome to head back to discover the truth, if you so wish.'

'I was going to visit Sir Wallace.'

'Me too. Perhaps, I can accompany you.'

Even though moments ago she had been angry with him, she nodded and they fell into step together.

'I apologise if I offended you with my talk on which husband to choose,' he said as they stepped into the castle.

'I wasn't offended. I was...' She paused, she couldn't tell him the truth, that the casual nature in which he talked about her with other men had made her realise he didn't care for her, and that had hurt something deep inside her, something that she wanted to deny was even there. 'It made it all the more real,' she said instead. 'By this time next week, I might be married to one of them, and I don't even know them.'

'I can see why that might upset you,' he said quietly.

They didn't speak again until they were in the tiny chamber she had reserved for Sir Wallace. He was pleased to see them, but he became tired quickly, and so they did not stay long. It was enough for Bronwen to be sure that the people she had assigned to look after him were taking their role seriously. She would arrange for them to have some extra coins for their efforts.

'I am going to spend some time with my mother now,' she said when Sir Wallace fell asleep in their presence.

'Very well,' said Sir Hugh, his head bowed.

'Would you...would you like to meet her?'

His head snapped up, his eyes meeting hers. She couldn't read his expression or tell whether she had crossed the line in asking him. 'I would be honoured,' he said eventually.

It was only after he'd accepted her offer that she realised she had been testing him. If he had said no or treated the request with derision, she knew she would have thought less of him.

They wended their way through the castle and up the stairs of the large keep, past her own chamber and on higher until they reached her mother's rooms. Although not as richly furnished as her father's area of the castle, they were far more comfortable.

Her mother seemed startled to see Sir Hugh with her but quickly warmed to him as he knelt on the floor to greet one of her favourite dogs. She met Bronwen's eyes over his prostrate form and smiled, a proper one full of warmth, one Bronwen hadn't seen for a long time, and something in her heart twisted painfully. The more time she spent with Hugh, the more it felt as if he were bringing her back to life, his presence helping her reconnect with her mother and easing the loneliness that had plagued her for years.

'You did well in today's tournament,' her mother said to Sir Hugh, as they settled in front of the fire. It may be warm outside the castle walls, but inside the thick stone, it was cool and Bronwen was grateful for the flames that warmed her toes.

'It was an enjoyable morning,' said Sir Hugh, deflecting the praise; Bronwen noticed he did that often, as if he was unused to hearing how good he was. 'How long have you had this gorgeous girl?' he added, playing with the dog's ears. Caddy's eyes rolled back in her head at Sir Hugh's ministrations, and Bronwen didn't blame her; his firm touch looked like bliss.

Bronwen leaned back against the cushions and let the conversation between Sir Hugh and her mother carry on without any input from her. It was good for her mother to have someone to talk to; it brought some of the light back into her eyes. The afternoon passed with much talk and laughter, but gradually Bronwen said less and less as her eyelids began to feel very heavy.

She didn't know how long had passed before her mother's hand brushed over her forehead. 'You need to wake up, my lovely girl.'

'Oh…' She stretched, rubbing her eyes to dispel the sleepiness. 'I hope I wasn't asleep long.'

'Judging by the snores, I would say it's been a while.' Heat rushed over her skin. She hadn't really been snoring in front of Hugh, had she? But her mother laughed out loud, and any embarrassment she might have felt was forgotten in the joy of that sound. Bronwen hadn't heard it in so long.

Leaving, she brushed her mother's cheek with a kiss. Before she could pull away, her mother whispered, 'He's a good one, darling. Don't throw away an opportunity to be with a man like that.'

Bronwen squeezed her mother's fingers, trying to convey that her choice of husband was not focussing on who was the handsomest or the best fighter or even the one who would make her laugh but on the man who could give her stability, a good home and a place where she didn't have to pretend to be calm.

She did not want the tumultuous feelings Sir Hugh inspired, no matter how good they had made her feel over the last few days. Sir Hugh had the power to make her forget everything she had always wanted, and that was frightening.

Slowly, she and Hugh made their way back down the spiral staircase. She was leading the way, but she didn't get the impression he was in a hurry either. She was intensely aware of him as he moved behind her. She had no way of knowing whether he was looking at her or concentrating on where he was putting his feet, but she fancied she could sense his gaze on the nape of her neck, and her skin there begged for his attention.

'My mother appears to have enjoyed your company,' she said as they passed by another level.

'She is a good woman.'

'She is.'

Bronwen slowed even more. They were reaching her level, and she found she did not want to go any farther. Perhaps it was the wine or the summer's sun or the way she was relaxed for the first time in so long, but she wanted more than just Hugh's gaze on her skin. Her heart started to pound with the knowledge of what she was about to do. It was risky, it went against everything she held dear, and yet it felt so right. She paused outside a door, her fingers resting lightly on the handle.

'This is my chamber.'

'Don't open the door,' he said sharply, not sounding at all like himself.

She froze, her hand still in place.

'If you open that door,' he continued. 'I will follow you in, and I will finish what I started in the corridor earlier.'

Her heart triumphed at the knowledge that she hadn't imagined it; he had been about to kiss her. She'd been cheated out of it, but now she could know exactly what it would feel like to have his mouth on hers. 'I can step inside. You do not need to follow.'

He groaned softly. 'I do not wish to be tested because, in this, I will fail.'

For a long moment, they stood there, their shallow breathing all she could hear, the cool handle all she could feel aside from her racing heart. Her whole body was trembling. In the next week, she would have to make a decision, a sensible one, one based on years of practical thinking, but right now she was tired. Tired of always being good, of always trying to make the correct decision, tired of being lonely and wanting someone to fill that void.

When she was with Hugh, she forgot all of that. He made her feel whole, as if she had a friend and a confidant; she wanted to hold on to that feeling for a little longer and she yearned for something more... something that satisfied the deep craving within, a yearning she did not fully understand but one she instinctively knew Hugh would fill.

She pressed the handle down and opened the door.

Chapter Eleven

For a beat, she didn't think he was going to follow her, but then she heard his footsteps coming behind her and the soft click of her chamber door as he closed it. She walked over to the long window, unsure of what to do with him now that he was in her private space but knowing she did not want him to leave until he had soothed some of the need that was burning within her.

He followed her, and for a while they watched the people of the castle moving far below them. She felt the gentle press of the backs of his fingers against hers and she turned her hand. His fingers linked with hers, his thumb tracing the inside of her wrist, backwards and forwards, sending flickers of sensation spiralling up her arm, tightening her nipples and making her legs weaken. It was at once lovely and not enough.

She turned to face him and he tugged her away

from the glass, bringing their bodies nearly flush with one another.

'This is wrong,' he murmured, his breath whispering across her forehead.

'I know.' It was and yet it felt right. Still, she should remind them both. 'I have no intention of marrying you.'

'I know.'

'I just… I want…' Her fingers moved of their own accord, stopping when they were a hair's breadth away from the long column of his neck. 'May I touch you?' she asked.

He nodded briskly, the fingers of one hand coming up to hold her hip. She crossed the tiny distance between them and rested her fingers on his pulse; it was hammering beneath his skin, as hard and as fast as her own heart. Her thumb moved to the base of his throat and he grunted. It was heady and powerful, this desire, speaking to a place within she hadn't realised existed. His breathing became harsh.

'I want more,' she said, her voice unrecognisable.

He grunted. She turned her head up so that she could look at him. He was gazing down at her, his lips parted, eyes glazed.

'I want to know what it is like to kiss you,' she whispered. 'Is that so bad?'

He closed his eyes. 'You are to marry another man within a sennight.'

'I know but…' she breathed.

He nodded as if he too understood this craving for something that could not be. He lowered his face until their breath was intermingling. His strong hands slipped around her, his palms flat against her back. 'I have thought of little else other than this since I saw you on the path,' he said. 'I have imagined you opening yourself to me, giving me what you have not yet given another man.'

'I have thought of it too,' she confessed. 'I have imagined you taking what you want and leaving me gasping for more.'

He groaned and lowered his mouth to hers, placing the softest of kisses against her lips. His lips were dry and firm. 'So soft,' he whispered against her, 'so gentle.' His lips brushed hers again, firmer this time.

Her lips parted and he deepened the kiss, his tongue tangling with hers. It was unexpected but somehow wonderful. She responded in kind, encouraged by his groan. His arms banded about her, pulling her flush with his body, and there was no hiding his reaction to what they were doing.

She rocked against him and his movements became frenzied, one hand tilting her head for better access, the other running down her spine and over the curve of her buttocks. Not to be outdone, her own hands ran over his body, stealing into his hair, over his wide shoulders and his muscled arms.

She wanted to do this forever, but he was slowing, bringing his arms to her waist and kissing her gently until he eventually lifted his head and gazed down at her. His eyes were glazed, his hair standing on end, and a fierce possessiveness swept through her. She'd done that. She'd taken a man so in control and precise in his movements and changed the way he looked. She reached up to him to smooth some of the strands, but he was dropping his arms and stepping away.

'Where are you going?' She hated that her voice sounded plaintive, but the words were out before she could stop them. In that moment, she saw what he could reduce her to, and she loathed herself for giving into her basic instincts. She had known he would change her, and in a moment of foolishness she had allowed herself to forget.

'If I stay, we will do something we regret and you will have to marry me.'

Her spine snapped straight and her head lifted. 'I have given you no indication that I will go *that* far.' It was important he knew that she was not free and easy with her favours. She may have kissed him, but she would not spread her legs for him. That was only something she would do with the man she married.

His skin turned a deep shade of red, but she felt no pity for him. 'I...' he began. But she didn't let him finish.

'If a woman asks you to kiss her, it doesn't mean she wants to have a roll in the hay with you.'

'I know that.' Irritation sparked in his eyes, the haze of lust finally fading. 'But we were...' The hand gesture he made was crude but somehow still made heat burn inside her where there should be anger. 'We were getting carried away, and I thought that our instinct might take over. I can see that I was wrong.'

'I wanted to know what it was like to kiss a handsome man, but I was not proposing we marry. I made that clear.' It was important that he understood this. She had not changed her mind. If anything, the last few moments had reinforced her opinion. Sir Hugh was the only person she had ever met who had the potential to hold power over her. One more of those kisses, and she would not be able to resist him, despite what she was telling him. Once she was completely in his thrall, he would be able to destroy her, and as much as she might desire him, she would not allow that to happen.

But she needn't have worried. Whatever it was that she had said to him had changed his demeanour completely. He was no longer looking at her with desire.

His emotions had shut down, and he looked as calm and considered as he was before a competition.

'As you have said, repeatedly, that you do not wish to marry me, you do not need to tell me again. I have understood the message. If you will excuse me, I must return to the barracks.'

He turned on his heel and strode out of the chamber, not looking back and leaving Bronwen unaccountably bereft.

Chapter Twelve

Two days passed. Lord Geraint, recovering from days of excessive drinking and eating, kept mostly to his suite of rooms. He arranged for the knights to perform a series of tasks around the castle, fixing a few structural problems, building a new fence and training some of the pages and squires.

Hugh handed a large stone to John, who fitted it neatly onto the stone wall he was creating. Hugh had to admit John was far better at this than he. 'What do you think of Lord Geraint?' he asked as he handed another one over.

'The man's a halfwit and has no idea what a prize he has for a daughter.'

Hugh shifted uncomfortably. He was aware that John, who he liked and admired, held Bronwen in high regard. It didn't make him feel any better about what had transpired in Bronwen's chamber, a memory that made his body tighten even as his spine curled in shame. He was investigating her father and had used their growing closeness to interrogate her mother, and then he had kissed Bronwen as if his very existence depended on it. He was a miserable cur who was going straight to hell.

Lady Morwen had confirmed what he already knew, that the wealth of Ceinwen had increased after the arrival of Ioan ap Cadfael, but Hugh still didn't know what to do with this information.

He pushed thoughts of the afternoon to one side; there was nothing he could do about it now. He had to move on and get the mission over with before he did any further damage. He had spent the last two days avoiding looking at or interacting with Bronwen and had poured his energies into his investigation, the real reason he was here after all.

He'd found out that no one had a solid grasp of where Lord Geraint's wealth was coming from. From what Hugh could establish, the increase had appeared to coincide with the arrival of Ioan ap Cadfael, Lord Geraint's right-hand man. As far as he could tell, no one thought this suspicious. Everyone seemed to think that Ioan was efficient with his duties. Hugh could find no proof otherwise and it was frustrating in the extreme. He *had* to find out something further, something which actually proved one way or another whether the wealth was due to Ioan's management or something nefarious. He could not let Leo and Tristan down, could not be the waster his family clearly thought him.

'I think you're going to win.'

For one wild moment, Hugh thought John was talking about his mission. 'What?' he asked.

John smiled at him. 'Lady Bronwen's hand in marriage, I think it is going to be you who wins the tournament.'

'I...' Images flashed before Hugh—Bronwen, her dark hair spilling over a pillow, her eyes laughing up at him, a small girl, the likeness to her mother astonishing as she ran to him calling, 'Papa,' and of a son with his mother's dark hair and Hugh's eyes. The longing for that future was so intense it nearly brought him to his knees.

'Better you than Gwilliam,' John continued.

'Better anyone than him.' Hugh shifted on his feet as he realised that not one of the knights was good enough for her. Except, for perhaps, *him*. No, that was a dangerous route to go down, a route that would only lead to his misery.

'Isn't that the truth?' John chuckled and placed another stone in the wall.

Out of the corner of his eye, Hugh caught a flash of dark hair. It could belong to anyone, this was a busy castle, but somehow he knew it was Bronwen. He forced himself to bend down and select another stone, the muscles in his neck straining with the effort of not turning to look at her. If he saw her, he would be lost. He would do something foolish, like follow her into her chamber and kiss her, all the while knowing how wrong it was to do so. And yet, it didn't seem to matter how disgusted he was with himself, knowing that he had lost control of his willpower, that he'd been distracted from his mission and that he'd managed to insult Bronwen. If she let him know she'd welcome him back, he would follow her in a heartbeat.

The knights moving around the castle and performing tasks allowed Bronwen to make her way around the men to talk to them without the pressure of being watched intensely by her father. She avoided Hugh. She had to. If she thought about him for even a moment, all her good intentions went by the wayside. She wanted to apologise to him for the words she had said and to beg him to return to her chamber so that they could kiss some more. It didn't matter how many times she reminded herself that she did not want to be in thrall to any man, she could not get the memory of his mouth on hers out of her mind. So she avoided him and perhaps he was avoiding her too, because she only saw glimpses of him from a distance.

Her father decreed Sir Gwilliam the winner of the

first day of tasks, although what he had done that merited that reward, Bronwen wasn't sure. She hadn't seen her father today, and word had reached her that he wanted her to decide on today's winner. She already knew she was going to choose Sir John. He appeared to be the most sensible choice of husband for her. Another reason she was avoiding Sir Hugh was that she didn't want to pick him, and she knew, without watching him work, that he would be the best with his clear-headed competence.

It wasn't that she wanted to find the man she married physically repellent, she knew she would have to lie with him and that there needed to be, if not attraction, then at least a friendly rapport between them.

A man who overwhelmed her senses, who made her act as if there were no rules that bound her behaviour, had no place in her life. Someone like that could control her within days of the marriage and make her life miserable if he chose. She was not going to allow anyone that power.

So she walked amongst the men and chatted with them, and most of them were fine, nice even. None of them made her want to drag them into an alcove and press her body into theirs. None of them made her stomach flutter or made her want to take them to speak to her mother. Sir John appeared to be the kindest and was therefore the safest choice. Safe was best.

She was striding away from Sir Gwilliam, unable to avoid him completely, when she walked smack into Hugh. It had been the first time she had been close to him since their moment in her chamber, and it was the first time since then that she felt she could breathe properly again, surely a coincidence.

'You cannot seriously be considering Gwilliam as a potential husband,' he growled, a deep scowl marring his normally calm features.

She wasn't. The reason she'd been moving so quickly was to get away from Sir Gwilliam, but she was not about to share that with Hugh. 'I have to consider everyone here.'

'How do you decide who wins this part of the tournament?' His eyes widened. 'Is this how you are going to get the man you want?'

She nodded slowly. 'As you can see, my father is not here, so I can report on what I want.'

'What about his right-hand man? Isn't he here in your father's stead?' Hugh nodded to the man loitering around the courtyard, watching the proceedings with keen eyes.

'Ioan ap Cadfael doesn't care whom I marry. He is only pleased we are getting this work done without having to spend extra coin.' That was true. Ioan's presence made her uneasy, she had a sense he was more dead than alive, and she avoided spending any time with him. Likewise, he showed no interest in her. He may be close to her father, but who she married would have no impact on him.

'I think the amount being spent on feasting more than makes up for it.' Hugh hadn't taken his eyes off Ioan, his expression intense.

'My father will think the coins parted for feasting will be well spent. He enjoys nothing more than making merry.'

Hugh scratched his cheek. 'Does your father do this often?'

'He has never held a tournament to get me wed before, no.'

Hugh rolled his eyes. Butterflies erupted in her stomach at the crack in his calm façade. She pressed her stomach, trying to rid herself of the unwelcome sensation. She had finished noticing how he looked, or rather, she had finished *reacting* to how he looked. They were not quite the same thing, but she was working hard on the former becoming true.

'I meant, does he hold these large feasts often?'

'As often as he can, yes. Although it is rare for so many of the castle inhabitants to be involved. He prefers to eat and drink with his select circle of men.'

Hugh opened his mouth, his shoulders hitching, but he shook his head, halting whatever words he'd been about to say.

'What?' she asked.

He shook his head again. 'I was about to ask you an impertinent question, but I managed to stop myself before I completely ruined our...' He shrugged and Bronwen didn't press him on what it was he thought he might ruin.

'You can ask.' She wanted to know what he was thinking, even if it made her like him more, especially if it made her like him less.

He let out a long breath. 'I warn you, it is intrusive.'

'You can't not ask me now. I will only follow you around until you tell me.'

He cocked his head, his eyes twinkling in the way she enjoyed too much. 'I won't tell you then.' He grinned as she growled in frustration. 'Fine.' He scratched his cheek again. 'I was wondering how your father affords to live this way. The only person I have heard of such extravagant living is the king.'

'I...' she paused. Was the amount her father entertained so unusual? She was used to it. It was part of life here at Ceinwen. It had never occurred to her that other strongholds might not feast regularly. 'Are you sure? How many castles have you lived in?'

'Only two but...'

'But?'

He scratched the top of his head. 'You are right, I

do not have enough experience to know whether your father is the norm or not.'

She nodded, but she did not feel as if he was satisfied with his answer. She should move on, but she couldn't. 'The land around Ceinwen is fertile and the seas are full of fish. We are wealthy, but I don't think the way we are is anything out of the ordinary.'

He was nodding as she was speaking, but she got the impression he wasn't really paying attention to her words. It was disappointing behaviour from a man she had considered different from everyone else.

Over in the far corner of the courtyard, Sir John leaned back and surveyed a wall he had fixed, a wide smile of satisfaction crossing his face. Hugh followed the direction of her gaze. 'He's a good man,' he commented. 'He'd make a fine husband.' For some reason, that annoyed her even more than him telling her to avoid Sir Gwilliam. Who she did or didn't think about marrying was not up to him.

'Like I said, I am considering everyone.'

'You're not considering me,' he countered quickly. 'You told me so on the first day and most days since, and then in your...' he trailed off, and her skin heated at the reminder of when they had last spoken.

'You certainly did not look upset when I told you I wanted a husband who would inherit his own castle on that first day. You told me you intended to leave here a wealthier man. Do you *want* to be considered?'

That wiped his expression clean. She folded her arms, gazing up at him. 'I...' he managed.

'You...'

'I liked kissing you,' he blurted out, a fiery red coating his cheekbones almost immediately. 'Forget I said that. Of course, you're right. I do not want to be considered. I am happy to win the prizes and then leave you to your perfect spouse.' He nodded to her and made to move away before stopping again. 'You still mustn't consider Gwilliam. He is not a good man.'

With that he strode away, leaving her gaping after him.

Chapter Thirteen

Hugh rounded a corner and stopped. Leaning against a wall, he groaned. What had he been thinking? He *liked* kissing her! Who said something as asinine as that? A child? A man who had no experience with women whatsoever? A man with no wits? All of those? Certainly a man with any dignity would not. What had possessed him to blurt out the truth like that?

Besides, she knew he had enjoyed kissing her. She had been there, had experienced the heady rush and the draw between them. He knew she had been as caught up in the moment as he had. He also knew it had meant nothing to her. She had made that very clear. She had wanted to test the desire that lay between them, and in the moment he had been powerless to refuse her. She had wanted him and he had wanted to please her.

She had been wild and passionate, and then she

had all but told him to go away when she was done with him.

He should be grateful. She had been honest with him at least. Unlike his experience with Lady Ann, Bronwen had made it clear where she stood from the very beginning.

The moment he had stepped into Bronwen's chamber, he had damaged his integrity. Now he would always know what it was like to hold Bronwen in his arms and would have to endure the eternal torture of never doing it again. He'd kissed Bronwen knowing he was possibly going to destroy her family, kissed her knowing there would be no future for them, and just now he had tried to interfere with her choice of husband when it was clear she did not want him to meddle, because everything that was happening to him could change the plans he had held dear for so long.

He rubbed his hand down his face. He'd expected this mission to test him, but he had not factored in what it was doing to his character. Each day, he had to question his principles, had to do things he was uncomfortable with and had to hide his true self from a woman he was thinking about with alarming frequency.

That he enjoyed this slide into a very different life from the one he had thought he wanted should worry him, but he was finding it increasingly hard to re-member a time when all he had thought about was excelling at a campaign. Being in a castle with other men who not only listened to him but respected his viewpoint was good, great even. He enjoyed it when the other knights sought him out to ask for his help. He got pleasure out of teaching different skills and even loved the shots of something powerful which seemed to hit his heart every time he caught sight of Bronwen. In short, castle life, something he'd once thought he abhorred, was something he was coming to enjoy.

It was not the life he and his brother knights had planned, and he knew he couldn't come to want it, but there were moments when he could see this sort of life for himself clearer than he could being on end-less campaigns. He'd always thought of the plan to try to join the King's Knights as Leo's idea. He'd gone along with it because of how much he valued Leo and Tristan's friendship, but it had never been his passion, and now doubts were creeping in. Doubts that he had to keep squashing, because if he truly did not want to become one of the most renowned warriors in the land, what did he want?

Images of Bronwen laughing and smiling up at him hit him and he sucked in a quick breath. This way lay danger.

He straightened, scrubbing a hand over his face. He needed to forget these dangerous thoughts. There was no future for him and Bronwen, and he need not speak to her again. It was obvious she knew nothing about her father's less salubrious dealings. Her innocence and naivety had shone through when she had suggested the wealth at Ceinwen was due to the fertile land and the fish in the nearby sea. The idea that the extravagance shown by Lord Geraint was normal behaviour was staggering, but he supposed she had never travelled and knew nothing about the world outside the castle walls.

He pushed himself away from the wall. He and John had finished their task. He'd been going to check on Wallace when he'd been distracted by the sight of Bronwen smiling politely at Gwilliam, and something sharp and jagged had lodged itself in his chest. The man was worse than her father and…and he'd already broken his promise not to think about Bronwen any more, barely a handful of moments after he'd made it.

He strode towards Wallace's chamber. The man was doing well, and hopefully he had passed the dangerous part of any break, the fever that might set in after such a serious injury. The only problem now was the boredom.

Hugh had almost reached the small room when he caught the flash of purple, the same colour Ioan ap

Cadfael favoured in his surcoat. Without thinking, Hugh followed.

Inside the castle, Ioan led him down a series of corridors, each one narrower than the last, until finally Hugh heard the clunk of a heavy door closing. He stopped and listened, but there were no more sounds. There was also nowhere for him to hide, so if he leaned against the door to hear what was going on inside and was caught, there was no way he could explain himself, the mission would be over. But was it worth it to find out what was going on behind the door? For the first time since he'd arrived, Hugh missed his two friends. They'd both have advice. Leo would probably tell him to go for it, while Tristan might urge caution. Either way, whatever they said would have helped him to plan his next move.

He edged closer to the door. Inside came a thud and then the sound of something heavy being dragged across the floor. The sound gradually became louder, suggesting Ioan was moving whatever it was towards the door.

Hugh turned and ghosted away from the room. He'd finally got a lead to follow. It may not be much, but it was more than he'd had before. Although he had no idea what was behind that door, he was going to find out. This was a good development; whatever was in there had nothing to do with Bronwen. He could move forward with this mission without speaking to her, and the sense of loss he was feeling was absurd. It couldn't have anything to do with her. He'd only known her a handful of days and would not miss talking to her.

He would keep telling himself that until he believed it.

Chapter Fourteen

The day of the planned hunt dawned with a low mist that shrouded the ground. Hounds ran among the horses' legs, causing Bronwen's mare to skitter sideways as they snapped at each other. Her knees brushed against the knight next to her; the young man turned an unhealthy shade of red before stuttering an apology.

'It was my fault,' she said, forcing a smile. 'I didn't have tight enough control on the reins.'

That long sentence proved too much for him, his mouth opening and shutting like a silent frog.

Behind him, Hugh watched the exchange, an amused glint in his eyes, a glint she was determined to ignore. The young knight moved away from her to join some of the other men. She let out a long breath, running her hands over the soft hair of her mount. She was trying to show an interest in all of the knights competing for her hand in marriage, but it was proving harder with some. If she was honest, it was proving harder with anyone who wasn't Hugh. None of them made her stomach flutter or her heart race, not like he did, and that pull to him was still there no matter how much she tried to pretend to herself otherwise.

'I think Godwin was intimidated by your beauty.' While she'd been concentrating on calming her horse, Hugh had moved nearer. He was close enough now that she could lean over and touch the sleeve of his shirt. The material looked impossibly soft as it clung to the muscles of his arm, muscles she was doing her best to overlook.

'I think he is probably just young,' she commented, not willing to be drawn in. Anything she said about them either appeared disingenuous or smug; neither were attractive personality tributes.

'He's older than me.'

Bronwen laughed but stopped when Hugh raised an eyebrow. 'No!' She looked over to where the knight had gathered with friends. 'But...'

'I'm not sure whether this is an insult or a compliment.'

She glanced between the two of them. Where Sir Godwin looked as if he was a year's worth of solid meals from developing the frame of a man, Hugh's wide shoulders looked as if he had been carved from an oak tree, solid and sure. Where the other man wasn't able to say more than a few words, Hugh spoke as if he could command an army. The comparison between them was unfair because it was so favourable towards Hugh, who she was not meant to be considering as a future husband but to whom she was continually drawn like a bee to pollen.

'Are you joining us for the hunt?' Hugh asked.

Bronwen thought that was rather obvious, as she was seated on top of her horse. 'I am.'

'Is it safe for a lady?'

Bronwen arched an eyebrow at him. 'I am a skilled rider.'

His lips twitched. 'I am sure that you are, and my words are not meant to offer an insult, only these damned dogs should be kept under control and not allowed to run about the horses' legs like this.'

'I agree, and it is not like my father's master of the hunt to act in such a way. I fear he is responding to my father's less sensible orders.'

'Which are?'

'Oh, I'm not certain that he has made any, but it would be like him to want the dogs to deliberately upset the horses. He would say it is to test the skill of the knights, to see which ones can best control their animals, but the truth is he enjoys chaos, or at least watching chaos ensue. I'm afraid he finds it amusing.'

Hugh studied the hounds as they weaved in and out of the crowd. For once, Bronwen was able to read his expression in the deep frown that marred his forehead. Hugh was obviously disgusted at her father's behaviour, and she could not blame him. How many times during this contest could her father's actions bring her shame? 'I will speak to the master of hounds and get him to rein in the animals.'

She made to move off, but before she could go anywhere, the horn for the start of the hunt sounded and the dogs broke off, dashing towards the forest, finally showing the discipline Bronwen was used to seeing.

The knights set off after them. Bronwen expected Hugh to race after them too, but he seemed content to ride alongside her, and she followed at a more sedate pace. 'Your father is a complicated man,' he said as they rode into the treeline and out of the sun. 'Has he always enjoyed stirring people up?'

'As far back as I can remember, yes.' There was no point in hiding the way her father was. Hugh had eyes, he could see how her father acted, and it was not a secret the family could hide. Her father wouldn't want to anyway; he was proud to be so affluent he could afford to feast and live the way he did.

'That must be very difficult for you and Lady Morwen to live with.'

Bronwen startled. No one had ever expressed sympathy for her or her mother. Not even her brothers, who knew what her father was like, who were good men but who had left her alone to deal with their father and not returned in years. Without her permission, her heart tumbled a little bit more in *like* with Hugh. She couldn't name it *love*, because falling for him, even a little bit, would be a complete disaster. She cleared her throat, 'It has not been easy.'

'My family is…challenging also.' Hugh clicked his tongue, keeping his horse on track with a simple command.

'How so?' She'd known this already, he had already mentioned it, but she wanted to know more. They were following the rest of the men, but at a distance. Bronwen should ride ahead, but she was interested in Hugh's background and did not want to increase her pace.

'I told you that when my brother came to the castle in which I was training, he did not recognise me.'

'You did.' She hadn't been able to believe it then, but now that she knew more of him, she was even less convinced. He had such a commanding presence she could not imagine anyone forgetting him.

'My whole family, the one I was born into, are singularly uninterested in me.'

'I find *that* very hard to imagine.' The words burst out of her before she could consider them, but she didn't regret it, not when a hint of a smile crossed his lips.

'Unfortunately, it is true. As you have pointed out already, I am a third son.'

'I remember.' She wished she hadn't been quite so blunt when she had told him so. Perhaps she was more like her father than she had ever believed.

'I am the seventeenth child of my parents.'

'Goodness.' Such numbers were not unheard of, but Bronwen couldn't imagine going through that many pregnancies herself.

He grinned. 'Quite.' His smile faded as quickly as it had appeared. 'Although not all my parents' children survived to adulthood. You can imagine that by the time they had reached me, they were tired of raising children. That task fell to my older brothers, who found me equally onerous. They were pleased when it was time for me to go away to train as a page.'

Bronwen's heart ached, imagining a young Hugh alone and facing an unknown world.

'Was the castle you were sent to a friendly place?'

He barked out a laugh. 'No. It was worse than my family's home.'

'Oh.' Something inside of her twisted. In all her plans for the future, it hadn't occurred to her that she might move to a place that was worse than her current situation. How naive! Her chest tightened and she pressed a hand to her ribs, trying to loosen the sensation.

'Are you all right, milady?'

'Of course. I...' She didn't want to share her current revelation. Besides, she wanted to hear more of his story. 'How was it worse?'

The rest of the hunt was moving farther away. It was getting hard to catch glimpses of the riders amongst the trees. They were unlikely to lose them as the sound of so many men, dogs and horses crashing through the woodland was as easy to follow as it was likely to scare away the very animals they were chasing. Bronwen made no move to get closer to them; neither did Hugh. She should, she knew that, but it was Hugh whose company she craved, Hugh whose blue eyes lit a spark within her and Hugh whom she wanted to kiss again, even though she knew she shouldn't.

'The lord of castle hated the pages and squires who trained there, but he had a special well of loathing for me and my closest friends. He'd been a good knight in his day, but not excellent. Now he has the reputation for producing some of the best knights in the land, which he doesn't want to lose, but he also cannot reconcile the fact that he was not, and now never will be, as good as the young men he trains. He made Leo, Tristan and I do the worst of the chores.'

He grinned. 'Now that I am describing it, it doesn't sound that bad.'

'You had friends.'

'Aye.' He transferred his reins to one hand, his long fingers curling around the straps. 'I've told you about them before, two good men, boys when we met obviously.' He used his free hand to push his hair from his forehead, his eyes were dancing at an unseen memory. 'Leo was a puffed-up fool when we met. Tristan and I nearly didn't bother with him, but there was something endearing about how hard he was trying to be good at everything.' He chuckled softly. 'I can't remember how it happened, but the three of us became close. They became my family.'

A sharp twinge of jealousy hit her in the chest, which was strange because she'd had brothers who were good men. Perhaps because they weren't close. She was sure her eyes didn't twinkle when she thought about them.

Hugh was still grinning. 'I've remembered.'

'Remembered what?'

'The incident that made us all friends. I can't believe I forgot it really.' He guffawed. 'Poor Leo.' He was laughing properly now.

'You can't leave it at that. What happened?'

'Leo believed he was the best sword-fighter in the castle. In fairness to him, by the time the three of us were knighted, he was but eight—' Hugh shook his head '—the practice sword was bigger than him. He was swinging it around wildly, waving it around, trying to disarm me. He tells me I was looking at him with a cool disregard.'

'I can imagine.'

Hugh raised an eyebrow at her comment.

'You always appear to be watching events in that way.'

They rode in silence for a moment, the only sound the fading noises of the hunt. 'I've always tried to appear calm. Leo is hot-headed and Tristan is not much better. By default, I became the composed one of our trio,' he said eventually. 'However, that's not necessarily how I feel.'

Before she could question him more about that, he continued. 'On this occasion, Leo began to move the wooden sword above his head. Because it was so heavy, he lost his balance and began staggering all over the practice ground. He still wouldn't give up, which may have been fine. Perhaps he would have eventually succeeded if it hadn't been for the trough.' Hugh laughed again. 'He seemed to fall for ages. The look on his face is something I always try to remember if ever I am feeling sad. It never fails to make me laugh.'

'Is this the same man who threw the bucket of piss all over himself?'

Hugh tipped back his head and roared with laughter. 'I'd forgotten I'd told you about that.' His eyes sparkled with mirth. 'Yes, that's the same person, but the incidents were many years apart. Although now that I think on it, it is always Leo who gets himself into messy predicaments. I think because he approaches everything with a level of enthusiasm that is mostly effective but sometimes goes horribly wrong. In the case of the trough, he was head-to-toe in muck. If he'd blustered or become angry, then that friendship would have died before it had begun, but he looked down at himself and laughed so hard he couldn't push himself out. I tried to haul him clear, but he was so slippery, Tristan had to help. After that, the three of us became close friends. Leo is a brilliant fighter, but he's often impetuous. Tristan is handsome and clever, but sometimes his charm gets him into trouble.'

Bronwen loved this insight into young Hugh's early years. 'How so?'

'Other people find it frustrating that Tristan doesn't seem to have to try hard to get what he wants. It incites hatred, and he has made enemies from it, which is grossly unfair.'

'People don't like him because he is handsome and charming. Is there really nothing else wrong with him? I can't imagine deciding anything about any-one based on the way they look.'

'Then you are unusual.'

She was also lying. She had judged Hugh on the way his intense blue eyes had settled on her. She thought about the way his hair stood on end when he ran his hands through it and how wide his shoulders were, and the judgements she had made had all been positive.

'Other women are not so discerning.'

'Well, they should be. A man should be judged on his actions, not on the way he looks.' She was not only a liar, she was also a hypocrite, but what she said seemed to have pleased him.

He turned back to face the way they were heading, a soft smile playing on his lips. She watched him, her heart growing lighter. He didn't have to tell her that women had passed him over in favour of his more handsome friend, it was obvious in his reaction. Bronwen couldn't understand it. With his square jawline and mesmerising blue eyes, he was, without doubt, the most attractive man she had ever met.

'Your eyes are burning into me. I can sense you want to ask me a question. What is it?'

'I...' She squirmed in the saddle. The noise from the hunt sounded from very far away. 'Perhaps we should hurry up and join the others.'

'Yes, we should.' But neither of them kicked their horse into quicker motion, continuing to pick their way through the undergrowth at a steady pace. 'Whatever it is, you can ask,' he said after a while.

'I'm wondering who she is and what she did.'

He straightened. 'Who?'

'The woman who chose him over you.'

His eyes widened slightly. 'How do you know there is someone?'

The burn of jealousy swirled in her stomach. She'd guessed there must be someone in Hugh's past, but she found she did not like the confirmation of it. 'It's in the way you talk about Tristan's looks. You love your friend, but there is a hint of bitterness there too.'

He shook his shoulders as if trying to loosen something within him, perhaps he was unaware that he was holding on to tension regarding his friend, but it was better that he knew. A woman who came between friends was not a person to hold in a heart. She waited.

'There was a woman, but she… She was the daughter of the lord of the castle in which Leo, Tristan and I trained. I have told you before that the lord hated us because we were better than him at most things.'

A laugh gurgled out of her. 'And modest too, I see.' He grinned and Bronwen tightened her grip on her reins to stop herself from reaching out to touch him. 'I did not mean to interrupt. Please carry on.'

'Lord Ormand hated us, and so it was highly unlikely he would allow me to marry Lady Ann anyway.' All Bronwen's mirth died. The idea that Hugh had considered marrying someone ate away at her insides, even though that had been an impossible dream for Hugh.

'But I was a young man and I was a fool for hope and I fancied that love would conquer all objections.' The burning became a flame at the mention of *love*. 'I should have known it was not me in whom Lady Ann had an interest. She never showed any desire in wanting to…er…touch or kiss or anything that a young woman might do to show favour to a man.' Now the burning was spreading to Bronwen's skin because she had shown that interest in an intense way that she could not hide or take back. 'Lady Ann did seek me out and appear to listen to me talk, and that was… exhilarating, I suppose. No one other than Leo and Tristan had shown much interest in me before that.'

Perhaps Bronwen was sickening for something; that was why her stomach and now her chest hurt. It could not possibly be because of the man who rode beside her, because if it was, it was time for her to ride away. She did not want to feel, did not want anyone to have the power to hurt her, even if she was expe-

riencing these feelings in sympathy. It was the opposite of what she had always wanted. She yearned
for calm, to only feel contentment, and the feelings
inside her were very far from that. She knew all this
and yet it seemed impossible to move her horse faster
to catch up with the others. She desperately wanted
to know more. 'How did you find out that it was not
you whose company she sought?'

'Ah. That took me far longer than it should have
done. I'm normally a good judge of character, but in
this I was blind. In fact, I was one of the last people in
the castle who figured it out. I was not the only man,
you see, who had an infatuation with Lady Ann.'

'You said "love" before.' Although why Bronwen
was reminding him of that, she had no idea. She certainly did not want him to say it again.

'Yes, I did, and that was because that's what I
thought I was experiencing. Now I know it wasn't.'

'How so?' Was it Bronwen's imagination or did the
forest seem lighter? Perhaps the sun was finally able
to penetrate the canopy of leaves overhead. Whatever
had happened to the air around them had appeared
to cure her of her sickness too.

'If I had truly loved her then I would have mourned
the loss of her and not concentrated so much on the
pain of my humiliation. You see, Lady Ann was in
love with Tristan.'

'Oh no.'

He grinned at her, not looking at all heartbroken. 'Indeed. There was another man who was in love with her.'

'This has the makings of a tragic play.'

Hugh laughed. 'More like a comedy. Lady Ann chased poor Tristan around the castle. Robert chased her. It was all very ridiculous and overblown.' He sobered. 'Although it did end badly, Robert was so convinced Tristan would steal Lady Ann from him that he framed Tristan, and me and Leo for good measure, for a crime.'

'How so?'

'To shorten a story that would take most of the day to tell, I shall begin very near the end. Lord Ormand had commissioned a monastery to produce a beautifully illustrated manuscript. It took over two years to make and was to be a gift to the king. When it was finished, it was stored at Lord Ormand's stronghold until such a time as the king was back in England. Whilst in his possession, it sustained heavy water damage. Robert claimed to have proof it was the three of us who committed such a terrible crime. It was… awful.'

This time, Bronwen didn't stop her urge. She reached out and brushed her fingers along the back of his hand. His skin was warm and dry. He loosened his grip on his reins and turned his palm towards her. She trailed her fingers along his hand until they were interlinked with his. He gazed down at where their hands were interlinked, saying nothing. The touch was probably not a good idea, but she wanted to show her solidarity. At least, that's what she told herself.

'What happened then?' she asked.

'We were punished,' he murmured, still looking at her hand in his. The difference in size was startling; his hand dwarfed hers, large and powerful, and yet she felt completely safe.

'How so?'

He lifted his head, his look pained. They had drifted closer in the last few paces, and now she could see clearly into the depth of his eyes. They were bluer than the ocean on a summer's day. They were framed with thick dark lashes that somehow enhanced the colour. She felt like she could read his soul in them, and right now it was clear he wanted to kiss her again.

She leaned towards him, her skin tingling, her lips craving his touch. His gaze flicked to her mouth and back to her eyes. His grip on her hand tightened, and he pulled her towards him, his eyes flashing with triumph when she did not resist. She could smell him now, a mixture of soap and wood smoke and fresh air. His breath whispered across her cheek, his thumb traced the inside of her wrist, and sensation scattered up the length of her arm. The world around them stilled; everything else ceased to exist. He came towards her, his movement deliciously slow. Her eyes fluttered shut, the whole of her being centring on the feeling in her lips, that deep craving that would be satisfied by nothing other than his touch.

A deer burst through the trees behind them, shattering the peace. Bronwen's horse reared in alarm, tearing her hand from Hugh's. He grabbed hold of her reins, tugging the panicking horse away from the path of the stag. More deer were crashing after it, their eyes wide as they leapt over fallen logs and twisting roots. Bronwen's horse was bucking, trying to throw her off and get far away from the distressed herd. Only Hugh's firm grip, kept that from happening.

The rest of the hunt followed the animals, charging over the ground, calling to one another as the hounds snapped and snarled. So intent were they on their prey that they barely spared a glance at Hugh and Bronwen, who watched as they all piled past, pushing and shoving one another to get to the front of the pack.

It was all over in moments, the noise of them moving away as quickly as they had appeared, but her horse continued to try and buck her off, even when the threat had gone.

Bronwen held on, her thighs gripping the mare, one hand on the saddle.

'I'm going to…' Hugh didn't continue his explanation before he leapt from his saddle to join her on hers. His large arms wrapped around her and she fell flush against him, her back against his chest.

There was no time to think about his strength as her horse began to renew her efforts to get both riders off. The mare was no match for Hugh's skill. As the horse started to calm her actions, Hugh jumped to the ground and came to her front. Bronwen couldn't hear what he was murmuring to the animal, but gradually it was soothed and all its movement came to a stop, although it was still breathing heavily and sweat coated its long neck.

Bronwen's grip on the reins was so tight, she feared the strap may be permanently attached to her fingers.

'Bronwen, are you able to get down?'

Bronwen shook her head; she would never be able to walk again.

'Can you take your foot out of this stirrup?'

She shook her head again, not able to find the words to tell Hugh that she would never move.

During those few short moments, she had really thought the mare would throw her to the ground and that she would be trampled on by the knights trying so hard to secure her hand in marriage that they would not stop to see to her safety. Everything inside her was frozen with terror.

Hugh's large hand wrapped around her ankle. Even

through her skirts, she could feel the warmth of his skin. He pulled her free of the stirrup before rounding the horse and doing the same with her other foot. Gently, he reached up and untangled the reins from her fingers, and then, as if she weighed nothing, he lifted her from her saddle and set her down on the ground.

Her knees nearly gave way and his arms came around her, holding her up. 'I've got you,' he murmured into her hair. 'Everything is all right, you are safe.'

Her body began to tremble, whether in shock or whether in reaction to his nearness, she didn't know. All she was sure of was that she couldn't move. As if sensing that, Hugh lifted her again before carrying her to the foot of a large tree. He sunk to the ground, leaning his back against the trunk and settling her between his legs. The gesture was intimate, caring and wonderful. She knew it was wrong, knew that they were crossing an invisible line once more, but in that moment, she did not care. She rested her cheek against his chest, and his chin settled on the top of her head, his arms coming around her in a gesture that had nothing to do with protection and did not feel like comfort either.

This was the way a man held his woman, and right then, Bronwen wanted that to be the truth.

Chapter Fifteen

Bronwen trembled in his arms, and the only thing that held Hugh back from riding after those men and making them suffer the consequences of frightening her was the fact that he could not let her go.

He'd been about to kiss her when the stampede had happened, had been so close to lowering his mouth and taking what was not his for the second time. It was just as well they had been interrupted. One kiss he could pass off as a brief loss of mind, a second time was intentional and left it dangerously open for a third. And he knew that if he kept finding reasons to kiss her, then he might as well give up his mission now, because he could lose himself in her.

The morning had been nothing like it should have been. He should have ridden with the other knights, should have found a reason to get close to the master of hounds. If he could get an ally within Lord Geraint's men, then this mission would be easier, he could finish sooner and he could get away from the temptation Bronwen presented.

Riding with her, telling her things that he'd not discussed with anyone ever should have set off a warning inside him. Hell, reminding himself of how Lady Ann had used him and had hurt him should have been enough to get him away from a woman who could hold an even greater spell over him. And yet...and yet, it hadn't. It had felt exactly right, as if she were the very reason he was here and not some mission that would determine his and his friends' fate. When he was with Bronwen, he was at turns fiercely attracted to her and absolutely content.

Bronwen was not for him, he knew that, but that did not mean that sitting here, with her head on his chest and his arms banded around her, was not the pinnacle of his life so far. Everything else, all his thoughts for the future, everything that had happened in the past, all faded away.

He knew he should keep his arms around her, wait until she had finished shivering and then help her back onto her horse before suggesting that they return to the castle and await the rest of the hunt. But the temptation to touch her, to commit parts of her body to memory was so strong. He fought to keep himself still, but his fingers twitched, and he knew he was losing the battle with himself.

He leaned his head back against the rough bark, relaxing into the hold. If she told him to stop, then he would. He would not touch her anywhere that was too personal, but if he could offer comfort in another way, then he would. Her hair fell over his arm in a golden wave. Before he could talk himself out of it, he bent his arm and brought his fingertips to the strands. It was as silky as it looked. Slowly, as not to alarm her, he twisted a strand around his fingers and gave it a gentle tug.

The weight of her pressed more firmly against him, and he took that as a sign that he could carry on with his exploration. He gathered more of it in his hand and let it fall through his fingers, watching as it caught the dappled light that was pushing through the leaves. It was so beautifully mesmerising, but he doubted the movement was bringing her much comfort, and the only way he could justify pressing her against him was that it provided her with something.

Softly, he pushed the strands over her shoulder, revealing the nape of her neck and a patch of skin there that had held him in its thrall for days. He pulled in a shuddery breath at the sight of her soft skin and the short hair that curled there. He brought the pad of his thumb to the base of her neck and pressed softly.

Her breath hissed out of her and he paused, unsure if that was a good sign or not. When she didn't pull away, he applied the same level of pressure to the other side of her neck with two of his fingers and began to work his way up, stroking and squeezing.

The soft moan she made when his hand moved into her hair shot straight to his groin. He shifted slightly so that she would not feel the evidence of arousal, but he didn't stop.

He moved his hand down the length of her spine, keeping to the same rhythm. She went boneless against him, soft whimpers escaping from her lips every now and then. He kept to her back even as he craved the feel of her cheek, the length of her jaw, to the soft curve of her breast. He could not do that and keep them both innocent, because he would not stop there.

Time passed, ceasing to have any meaning. Maybe he would have continued until he died of starvation, but a whinny from his stallion broke the spell. From the distant hollering, it sounded as if the hunt were moving back in their direction.

'We should move,' he said gruffly.

She looked up at him, her eyes glazed, her lips parted, and it took all his willpower not to plunder her mouth with his own, but he still could not pull away. He wanted her more than he had wanted anything in his whole life, more than he wanted to breathe, and yet the sensible part of him, the part that had kept him in good stead his whole life, refused to let him lean forward and take what her eyes offered.

She might want him, might desire him as much as he did her, but she had told him repeatedly that she did not want to marry him. In that moment, she might want his body, but ultimately, she would not pick him, and he had already decided that he was not worthy to be her husband. And, he reminded himself, that was a good thing, because a wife at this stage of his life did not suit his long-term needs, no matter how much they might satisfy his short-term ones.

When she continued to gaze up at him, he shifted slightly, as if he were about to stand. 'The hunt might be heading back in our direction. We should head back to the castle so that we are out of their way. Unless you would like to join them.'

She shook her head, pressing her lips together as the look of desire faded from her eyes. 'No. I should like to return to Ceinwen. You may join them if you wish.'

'I should rather return you safely to the castle.'

'But you will not win this tournament.'

'I feel as if I already have.' The moment he said the words, he wished he could cram them back into his mouth. The statement was almost a declaration of intent, and yet he could not bring himself to take the words back. They were the truth after all, and he did love the truth.

She gazed at him for a long moment, but the sound of the hunt was growing ever nearer, and she finally pushed herself to her feet.

'I do not know why I was so scared,' she told him as she moved towards her mare. 'I have ridden many times before and have even been thrown off a time or two, but I truly thought my days were numbered.' He was grateful to her for keeping the conversation casual and not bringing up the fact that he had held her and caressed her as if she were the most precious thing in the world.

'Perhaps it was the chaos of the hunt, the frightened animals and all those men charging after the beasts.'

'I feel sorry for them,' she said as she ran a soothing hand down the length of her mare's neck.

'The men?'

'No. The deer.'

'You do? But it is part of nature. We must eat, and we will dine well this evening on fresh venison.'

'I know that we eat meat to survive, but must the animal face so much fear before it meets its end?'

'I hadn't thought of it like that. Here, let me help you.' He made a step from linking his hands together. She put a boot onto it, and he boosted her up into the saddle.

They made their way back to the castle; this time talking about animals and not touching on anything personal. He made no further confessions, nor did he bring the talk back to her father and the way he acted. He promised himself that he would start again as soon as he returned, that he would ride away from her and let her return to whatever it was she did every afternoon, that he would not think of her once. For now, he would enjoy her company, he would take this moment out of time and allow himself the joy of just listening to her talk, because once he found out the truth, he would not be able to do so ever again.

Chapter Sixteen

Sir Gwilliam had won the hunt. Bronwen had suffered through a whole feast with him sitting next to her, regaling her of every moment of the pursuit at which, according to him, he had excelled.

At first, her father had seemed enamoured with the verbose knight, whose inflated opinion of himself was only his second most unpleasant quality. The first appeared to be a penchant for cruelty, which came across in all the tales he told about himself. Bronwen worried that her father's interest might work against her. If he liked the man more than any of the other knights, then he might force her to marry him, and she would not have any say in the matter. But her father's attention soon wandered back to the contents of his wine goblet, and Bronwen was left to endure Sir Gwilliam by herself. Wedged between the two men, it was a strange sort of isolation. She was not physically alone, but she might as well have been given the amount of attention either man gave her. It was the exact opposite of her time with Hugh.

When Sir Gwilliam's tales seemed never-ending, she allowed herself the indulgence of thinking about her own experience of the hunt. She had been truly terrified when her horse had tried to buck her off. She had thought the men would not be able to stop their mounts had she fallen before them, and she would have been trampled to death. But her fear had soon turned to something else, something far more powerful.

As Hugh held her in his arms and kneaded her back, the world had seemed timeless. All her worries had ceased to exist as the cool breeze had brushed her skin, and the birds had sung high up in the trees above them. Everything she had ever told herself about what she needed from life had seemed utterly pointless in the beauty of Hugh's caress. For the first time in her life, she had felt treasured and wanted.

When they'd arrived back at the castle before the others, they had gone their separate ways. Hugh had gone to check on Sir Wallace, while she had spent time with her mother. She'd hoped the separation would rid her of the overwhelming pull Hugh seemed to have over her. It hadn't. If anything, being apart from him made the feeling worse.

Before the celebratory feast, she had felt desperate, that if she didn't see him soon, she would crawl out of her skin. But seeing him in the flesh hadn't made it better either because she hadn't been able to talk to him, wedged as she was next to Sir Gwilliam. She could only look at Hugh from afar. For some reason, he wasn't sitting with the other knights. Instead, he had found a place amongst some members of her father's household, and he was seemingly intent on what they were saying. He did not glance at her once. She knew that because she could barely tear her eyes away from him.

By the time the meal was over, she was desperate to return to her own chamber, but the minstrels began to play songs with an upbeat tempo, and dancing began. Her father got a second wind from somewhere and ordered everyone to join in. The steps were easy enough to follow, and normally Bronwen enjoyed losing herself to music as she was spun around the Great Hall, but this evening, Sir Gwilliam was the man standing to her right, and she had to hold his hand as they all danced in a circle. In reality, it was no different from the hand of the man on her left. If she closed her eyes, she would not notice the difference between the two, but somehow it felt as if the skin that touched Sir Gwilliam burned and itched. The minstrels began another song, and the crowd cheered in delight as a favourite began. More people were joining the circle, but Sir Gwilliam held on to her tightly until, in the blink of an eye, he was gone and another hand was taking its place.

She didn't need to look to know who it was; her body was reacting the way it always did when Hugh touched her, as if it were finally alive after years of being asleep. They moved to the rhythm of the music, their feet following the steps together, just the two of them in a hall full of people. She laughed, wild and free and so happy in this endless moment.

The song ended, the minstrels muttered something about taking a break, and the dancers broke into smaller groups, laughing and talking. Hugh kept hold of her hand, weaving through the people until the two of them were stepping outside into the cool night air. After the smokiness of the dimly lit hall, it was lovely to breathe deeply. Hugh paused for a moment before tugging her away from the large doors through which the revellers were still enjoying themselves.

He led her to a gap between the stables and the smithy, the two buildings unusually quiet in the stillness of the night. He came to a stop a few steps in. 'I know that you don't want to marry me and I know that this is not something we should be doing, but I can't seem to keep away no matter how much I tell myself to.'

Bronwen pressed her lips together. She was no longer sure it was true that she did not want to marry Hugh. She knew all her arguments as to why he was so wrong for her, knew that the way she was starting to feel about him was powerful and out of her control, knew that he could not provide her with what she had thought she always wanted, but she wasn't sure that mattered any more. When Hugh was looking down at her with such intensity, it was hard to remember any of the reasons.

'The thought of you married to that foul man...' Hugh's whole body shuddered with revulsion. 'It was all I could do not to kill him when I saw him holding your hand during that dance.'

Something inside her thrilled at his words. 'But you did not look at me for the whole meal.'

'I couldn't.' He closed his eyes, leaning forward until his forehead was touching hers. 'I don't understand what you are doing to me. I am always in control of my actions and now...and now I have dragged the most beautiful woman I have ever laid eyes on into a dank passageway just so I can have a few stolen moments with her. What is this?'

'It is worse for me.'

He huffed out a laugh, his breath caressing her forehead. 'How so?'

'I am meant to be finding a suitable husband, but

how can I look at any of the others when all I see is you.'

He sucked in a breath, sounding almost pained. 'I shouldn't do this,' he murmured.

'Do what?'

He brought his mouth to hers. This was no smouldering kiss. This was fire and heat, and it burned with the power of a thousand suns. His tongue danced with hers, and she threaded her fingers through his hair, the dark strands so soft to the touch. It was everything and it was not enough. She ran her hands over his broad shoulders, his chest, the length of his spine, everywhere she could reach, memorising how he felt beneath her touch. If this was the last time they kissed, it had to count.

He pulled her flush against him, and she could feel him against the whole length of her body. The hard length of him pressed against her stomach, and her soul triumphed, knowing that she had done that to him, that she had that power over him. It was heady and it was delicious, and she wanted this moment to never end.

She moved against him and he groaned into her mouth. His thumb brushed the underside of her breast, and it was her turn to moan as her nipples hardened into points. This is what she had been missing, this is what drove men and women to act in the way they did around each other. She understood now. His thumb inched higher. Even through the fabric of her dress, she could feel him. She arched towards his touch, and eventually he brushed over the spot which ached for him the most. She bucked against him, and he appeared to lose his mind. His hands were everywhere, caressing, pinching and driving her wild, and then abruptly he stopped.

'What?' she said. Her voice appearing to come from far away.

'There's someone nearby.' His voice was gravelly, as if he had not used it for a long time.

'I don't care,' she said, arching against him.

He closed his eyes as if in pain. 'You might to-morrow.'

He made a good point. She needed space away from him to really think about whether she was willing to change her mind about everything she had always wanted in her future husband, whether she really was willing to risk her heart and give in to this desire that burned between them.

'There are too many people here,' said someone, far closer than she had realised.

'It still needs to be done soon,' said another voice. She frowned; she recognised that person, but who was it?

'If we rush it, it could end badly. Any one of Geraint's guests could turn against us.'

'The tournament ends in two days. We'll act then.' That was Ioan ap Cadfael. That's how she knew the voice.

'Very well,' said the first man, whose voice she recognised but could not place.

'Until then,' said Ioan.

She and Hugh waited in silence, but there was nothing more said, and presently they heard the two men walking away, although they appeared to be going in separate directions.

'What was that about?' murmured Hugh. He was still holding her tightly against him, but she could see that his desire for her had faded from his eyes.

'I'm not sure. Possibly it's to do with the collection of tithes.'

'Tithes?'

'Yes. You know when we collect produce from...'

'I know what tithes are, but why would you think that conversation was about that?'

She shrugged, unsure of why it mattered. The two men had not caught them kissing, and that was really all that was important. Lots happened in the castle that did not involve her. She was good at the things that did, but the delivery of tithes was a matter for the lord and his second-in-command, not the women. 'It is nearly time for the collection, but it has been put back because of the tournament.'

'I see.' But it didn't sound like he did, not really. 'We should return to the hall before someone notices we are missing.'

Bronwen didn't want to, she wanted to stay out here and discover why Hugh's attitude had changed, or she wanted to kiss again, but it was clear from the tone of his voice that he did not want to, and she would not force her attentions on anyone. 'Of course.'

He dropped his hold, and the cool air of the night rushed over her. She shivered and his arm came around her. 'It's fine,' she said shrugging him off. 'I'm fine.' If he did not want to hold her any more, then she did not want him to feel obliged to keep her warm.

They walked back to the Great Hall without speaking, and once inside, he bid her good night before disappearing into the crowd and leaving her with no idea as to what had just transpired.

Hugh had been so busy kissing Bronwen he had almost missed this latest development. He'd been so intent on his own pleasure that he had not been paying attention. He had lost himself in her, and his chest tightened at the thought of just how much he was keeping from her at the same time he was enjoying her kisses. He was a bastard who wasn't fit to walk into the same chamber as her, let alone hold her in his arms.

Hugh prowled around the edge of Great Hall, furious with himself. Everyone else was enjoying themselves as they had every evening since he had arrived. This gross display of wealth was sickening when he thought about other parts of the country who struggled to find enough food to put a full meal on the table. Hugh should be doing his bit to put a stop to it, but he wasn't, his mind too full of Bronwen. If he hadn't overheard those two men talking, he had no doubt he would have begged Bronwen to take him to her chamber, and then he would have been sunk.

Hugh leaned against a supporting pillar and gazed across the hall, seeking out Bronwen before he could stop himself. She was talking to Sir John, smiling up at him kindly. Hugh hated to admit it, but they were compatible. John was kind and gentle and would be a decent husband, and Bronwen would be a devoted wife who would look over his castle with the attention to detail she was good at. And it was not John's fault that Hugh now wanted to stride over and rip them apart.

He looked away. These thoughts were not doing him any good. He spied Ioan ap Cadfael in one corner of the hall. The man had obviously returned after the conversation he'd had in the courtyard. Hugh doubted that whatever he had been discussing had anything at all to do with tithes, but he was glad that was what Bronwen believed. It showed she was innocent of all knowing what was wrong at Ceinwen Castle. Ioan was now enjoying the company of a woman Hugh didn't recognise; his hands were sliding up beneath the woman's skirts, and they both had a giddy look on their faces, which suggested neither of them would be going anywhere soon. There may be time to rescue the evening and Hugh's mission after all.

He took one last look at Bronwen before he left the hall. Her golden hair burned bright in the candlelight, and he had to physically stop himself from crossing the room and taking her back into his arms. She was no good for his concentration, and so he turned away, his heart twisting as he did so.

The pain in his chest didn't lessen as he stepped outside. He was making a mess of this, and he was going to end up in a worse position than when he'd realised what Lady Ann was up to. At least Bronwen had been upfront about what she wanted from him. She wanted his body, and he was too much of a fool not to give into what simmered between them. What he needed to remember was that even if his mission did not exist, Bronwen was not going to choose him to be her husband, regardless of their shared physical passion. It was not enough for her; *he* was not enough for her. That should not hurt. He had learned early on in life that he would never be someone's first choice. Lady Ann had proven that lesson to him, and now Bronwen was doing the same, albeit in a much more direct manner. Yet, despite it being the most foolish thing imaginable, he was sore from the knowledge he was, once again, being overlooked.

He let himself into the castle walls. If anyone saw him coming this way, they would think he was visiting Wallace. He did so at least twice a day, but this time he was not here to see the young man. A couple of candles lit the corridor that led to Wallace's chamber, presumably for the castle servants who were looking after Wallace. Hugh took one down to light his way.

'Beeswax,' he muttered as his hands closed over it. 'That's in keeping.'

Of course Lord Geraint would have beeswax candles lighting corridors that weren't being used overmuch. No tallow candles for the wealthy lord, not even here. He lifted the candle to take it with him; he might need it to see what was in the locked room.

When he turned the corner, the small flame did little to light the space in front of him. Hugh moved slowly, careful not to extinguish the flame. It seemed to take forever to reach the chamber he had heard Ioan in a few days ago, but finally he was there.

It was the work of nothing to pick the lock. Ioan was clearly not expecting anyone to go in search of whatever was in the room and had not added anything other than the original safety features. Hugh, as well as all the other knights at Ormand's castle, had been taught how to get through locked doors, and it was only moments later that he heard the telltale click of the lock opening.

The door creaked on its hinges as Hugh slowly pushed it open. He waited a beat in case there was anyone inside, but when no sound of anyone breathing came from within, he stepped over the threshold.

The candlelight didn't illuminate the room well, but he had the impression that it was full from top to bottom with wooden crates. He began to walk around the room, methodically checking each one. By the time he reached the back of the room, his stomach was churning. So far, every crate he had looked in was piled high with weapons: swords, arrows and daggers. It was far more than necessary for arming this castle. Although there were many men here now, the normal level of soldiers was probably nearer thirty men, fifty at a push, but some of those would be farmers and would only be used to defend the castle if absolutely necessary.

The weapons in these crates were for an army.

Hugh moved on.

Another crate contained coins, more coins than Hugh had ever seen. The next one was the same.

He had seen enough.

He let himself out of the room and reset the lock.

He walked back along the corridor and replaced the beeswax candle in its nook.

He should go and speak to Wallace, but he didn't know what he would say. The wind had been knocked out of him by what he had seen this evening, and his mind was scrambling to make sense of everything he had seen and heard since he had arrived at the castle. He had so many questions. For which army were those weapons destined? Was it France, or had they been acquired to help the English army? Doubtful but possible. Was Lord Geraint involved? It seemed most likely, but the man did not come across as the sharpest of lords. It could be that his castle was being used as a place to store the weapons. It was only Ioan who had appeared to do anything that appeared suspicious. Even if Lord Geraint wasn't guilty of being involved, did the fact that it was happening in front of his nose make him guilty of treason, if that's what was being committed here?

He had no answers for any of those questions.

There were several things he knew to be true: The

wealth in that room was obscene. The weapons and coins could not be here via legal means. Ioan ap Cadfael was involved in whatever this was.

When it was all revealed, Bronwen was going to get hurt, and he could not bear the thought of it.

He sank to the ground, winded by the thought of her devastation. Nobody would want to marry the daughter of a traitor, and what would become of her then? Would she be thrown out of the castle? Perhaps she would have to join a nunnery. He groaned as he imagined the spark that made her who she was being slowly extinguished as she faced a lifetime of something she did not want.

There was one thing he could do for her, and that was to wait until after the tournament to reveal what he had found. It was a risk, but he had already heard those men talking about their plans. They were not going to do anything until after all the knights had left. He had time. Bronwen could marry and be away from here before the contents of that room were discovered. He could give her that.

Of course, that meant she could not marry Gwilliam. Once that man realised that he would not have access to a rich in-law, there was no telling what Gwilliam would do to his wife. Sir John was still probably the best choice. He was a good man, a little dull perhaps, but that was better than volatile. He was after a woman to run his household and bring his existing daughters up correctly. Bronwen was a good choice for him, and he was wealthy enough not to miss the connection to the Ceinwen fortune.

Yes, John would be a fine match. Hugh would help him win the melee tomorrow, and that would put him in good stead to win the tournament overall. It would be up to Bronwen then to decide whether he won the final task that she had yet to reveal to all the knights.

It could not matter that the thought of her married to another man, even one as innocuous as John, made him want to rage against the injustice of it all.

He had never been destined to marry Bronwen anyway, even if she had wanted him that way. This decision changed nothing, and there was no reason for his heart to feel as if it were cracking into millions of pieces. He would endure this, and he would move on and start again, as he always had done.

Chapter Seventeen

The melee was meant to be the grand finish to the week-long tournament, although Bronwen had her own challenge to go later that day. For the melee, the knights would split into two groups and fight against each other as if they were two sides of opposing armies. It was meant to be an entertaining spectacle, and the crowd was certainly geared up to enjoy themselves. Next to Bronwen, her father was vibrating with excitement.

'I expect to see some bloodshed today,' he crowed. 'Those two men of yours will fight to the end to be victorious.'

'What?' she gasped, twisting in her seat to look at her father. She had no idea that he had been paying attention to any of the tournament that didn't either involve violence or ale and wine.

'Don't play coy with me girl. I have eyes. Sir Hugh and Sir Gwilliam are the top contenders. Either would be a good match. They come from good families. Sir Hugh is tipped to go far.'

He'd said that before, but she wasn't sure what he meant. 'Go far?' she repeated dully.

'Yes. He is one of Lord Ormand's men. The lord's a jumped-up pimple, but he has produced some excellent knights over the years. The recent crop is meant to be even better than normal. Sir Hugh is expected to reach the very highest knights of the land.'

Bronwen couldn't have been more astonished if her father had suddenly declared he was never going to drink a glass of wine again. 'How do you know all this?'

He shrugged. 'Ioan told me. I can't have you married off to just anyone. We are one of the most prominent families in Wales and have standards to maintain.'

That sounded more like Ioan talking than her father, but Bronwen didn't comment.

'Sir Gwilliam is not as talented a knight, but his family's stronghold has a prominent position in England, and so we cannot dismiss him as an ally either. Yes, one of those men would make an ideal husband for you, and they both know it. It has been very enjoyable watching them try to outdo each other over the last few days.'

'I...' Bronwen floundered. She had no idea her father could still form this level of astute observation. 'What if neither of them win?' If her husband was not to be Hugh, then Sir John was still the most palatable of the other contenders. He had come close to winning some of the competitions, and Bronwen had declared him the winner when it had come to performing helpful tasks around the castle. He was a pleasant man. He would be a kind husband. There would be no yearning for his touch, but there would be a companionable relationship between the two of them. She would not burn for him and, in turn, he would never have the power to destroy all that made her who she was.

'Bah. One of them will win, and my money is on Sir Hugh. Sir Gwilliam wants to be allied to our wealth, but Sir Hugh wants you, and that is a more powerful motivator.' Her father glanced across at her. 'Don't look at me like that, you look like a fish.'

She clamped her mouth shut and turned her attention back to the fighting ground where the knights were assembling. Her mind was whirling. How had her father noticed so much? He was the most self-absorbed person she knew, and yet he had dissected the situation and come up with the truth. For all that she was shocked by her father's comments, she couldn't stop the thrill that ran through her at the idea of someone else noticing that Hugh wanted her.

The fighting began. From high above, it looked real, although none of the wooden swords drew blood. At first, it was a jumble of men, but gradually men dropped out if they were deemed to have been killed, and soon there were a few men left.

Bronwen should have been pleased that Sir John was one of the remaining men. It put him in good stead to win the whole tournament if she picked him as the winner of the final task tomorrow, but every time Hugh moved, she held her breath. She was willing him to win, even when that would make him the overall winner, even without her task. If he won, it meant she didn't have to make a difficult choice because it would already have been made for her. She wouldn't have to go against what she'd always thought she'd wanted for herself—a nice, unexciting man—and follow what she craved instead. Perhaps she was more like her father than she'd ever thought. He always did what he wanted, and to hell with the consequences. That wasn't her, or at least she'd always assumed it wasn't. This craving for someone who wasn't right for her was very much like her father and the way he seemed to have no self-control.

Below them, Sir John was knocked to the ground. Hugh turned to haul him to his feet. In that moment, Sir Gwilliam advanced on him, shoving another knight out of the way in his haste to get to Hugh.

'Watch out!' The warning burst out of her without conscious thought. But Hugh couldn't hear her over all the other hollering and jeering.

Bronwen held her breath as Sir Gwilliam neared, his sword raised, his lips twisted with malicious intent. And then, his blade was arching through the air, rushing towards Hugh's bent head. At the last second, Hugh twisted, diving away. Sir Gwilliam stumbled as his sword met only air. He righted himself, only to come at Hugh again, but Hugh was ready for him this time and easily defended his attack.

'See,' said her father, rubbing his hands together. 'They are going to fight each to the death all for the privilege of being my son-in-law.'

Bronwen didn't remind him that only moments ago, he'd told her that Hugh was after her, not the wealth of his estate. It didn't matter. Not in this endless moment of sword clashes. All around them, the fighting of the melee continued, but Bronwen did not have eyes for that. She was focused on Hugh and Sir Gwilliam as the two men battled.

Hugh had better technique, but he seemed to care that the men around them should not be hurt in the battle. Sir Gwilliam did not care. He swung his sword around with abandon, not seeming to worry if he hit a man supposedly on his side or not.

Her father cackled as one of his swipes smacked

into a man's side, sending him sprawling. That was the moment Hugh lost his careful control on his own movements and began to attack. Fury radiated from him as he rained down blow after blow that were impossible for Sir Gwilliam to counter.

Sir Gwilliam was falling back, the smug smile wiped from his face to be replaced by slack-jawed shock. Bronwen wasn't surprised. It was obvious now that Hugh had been holding himself back before this. His brute power was matched with precision skill. He was a force that could not be stopped.

Bronwen was up on her feet, cheering with the rest of the crowd as one final blow sent Sir Gwilliam sailing through the air, landing on the ground with an audible thud. The melee was still going on, but none of the other contests were as exciting as the battle between Hugh and Sir Gwilliam, and now that one of them was the victor, it was all but over in eyes of the crowd.

As Hugh turned, his gaze lifted and unerringly met hers. That now familiar bold look hit her chest, and she pressed her fingers to her lips. The moment seemed to stretch forever but was also over before she could blink and Hugh was turning back to Sir John to help him to his feet. The two men were talking and smiling slightly at an unheard joke. Almost all eyes were on them, but something caught Bronwen's attention, a movement where there shouldn't have been one.

'Hugh!' she screamed at the top of her lungs.

The crowd gasped as Sir Gwilliam ran at Hugh, a metal dagger glinting in the sunlight.

Where had that come from? Real weapons weren't allowed during the melee; it wasn't a fight to the death.

Bronwen screamed as the blade whipped through the air, Sir Gwilliam aiming for Hugh's exposed back.

Time slowed.

Sound ceased to exist.

Hugh spun, catching Sir Gwilliam's arm in a firm grip. Sir Gwilliam snarled, still trying to force the dagger down, now towards Hugh's throat.

Next to Bronwen, her father roared with laughter as if seeing a man's life in danger were the most amusing thing he had ever witnessed.

Bronwen could no longer sit by and watch this farce. She pushed and shoved her way through the crowd of spectators, trying to keep her eyes on the two men the whole time. Even though Sir Gwilliam was using all his weight to pin Hugh down, Hugh was still able to hold him aloft and to stop the blade from connecting with his throat. Why was no one stepping in to help him? There were so many of them, they could easily haul Sir Gwilliam away, and maybe that wasn't the knightly way, but it was sure as hell the better one.

Finally free from the crowd, she ran down the short flight of stairs, momentarily losing sight of the fight. A roar from the spectators had her stumbling before she righted herself again. Desperate to see what had just happened, she sprinted to the front of the stands.

The world spun as she spied legs spread wide on the ground before it righted itself to show that it was not Hugh who was lying there but Sir Gwilliam.

She crossed the remaining space on unsteady legs, and there Hugh was, kneeling with Sir Gwilliam's dagger in his hand, the man himself glaring up at him but unable to move due to Hugh's large hand on his shoulder.

She turned to Ioan who was watching the proceedings with the same detached air he observed everything. 'I want this man taken away,' she said, pointing at Sir Gwilliam. 'And I don't want him here any more.'

'I'll have him taken away now, but it is up to your father whether he leaves, not you.' Ioan gestured to some guards, who scooped Sir Gwilliam up and marched him towards the castle. It wasn't ideal, but it was better than nothing.

She inhaled a shuddery breath and took a tentative step towards Hugh. Men were slapping him on the back, grinning and congratulating him on taking on Sir Gwilliam and the way he had ended it so easily despite his disadvantage. The melee seemed to have been forgotten; no outright winner was being celebrated, although a few men were still standing, Sir John being one of them. Not that Bronwen cared; she had eyes only for Hugh.

While the crowd milled around him, Hugh looked up, his gaze unerringly hitting hers once more. For a long moment, they stared at one another, and then he nodded once.

She nodded back, the moment stretching endlessly between them.

Chapter Eighteen

Hugh stood gazing up at the keep. He knew which chamber housed Bronwen. Hers was one of the few rooms to have a long window. He wasn't sure, but he thought he might be able to see a flicker of candle-light through the warped glass. The pull to go to her was strong, so intense that he leaned back and pressed his fingers into the stone wall behind him as if that would somehow keep him in place. Nobody had won the melee outright, but in a moment of unwanted clarity, Hugh had suggested the winner be John, and that had become the accepted outcome. It put John, Hugh and Gwilliam as the men leading the tournament. Bronwen would probably marry John. He was the sensible choice, and if he weren't himself, he would probably suggest that's what she should do. But the reality of that decision burned something deep inside him, something he would never voice.

Bronwen had given all the knights the final task.

It was to compose a courtly love poem and perform it at the final feast tomorrow evening after which the winner would be announced.

He shouldn't even attempt it. Not because he couldn't, but because to enter the final contest was suggesting that he did, in fact, want Bronwen as his wife.

He closed his eyes, leaning his head back against the stone wall. The thing was, he could picture it, his whole life before him with Bronwen by his side. Or, if not by his side, then at least waiting for him at home, raising their children while he went on campaign. But among the myriad of problems this image conjured, it was imagining the place Bronwen and their children would be living. He didn't have anywhere for her to go. It was not like he could leave a wife with his family. They didn't care about him, so they weren't going to provide a place for his bride, and any offspring he had. This was what Bronwen wanted, the very thing she had stressed on the first day of the competition, and he doubted she had changed her mind because of a few passionate kisses and some heated glances.

That *he* was even contemplating marriage was such an outlandish idea that he should be rolling around on the floor laughing. Even when he'd been enamoured with Lady Ann, the thought of marrying her hadn't truly crossed his mind except as an idealised fantasy that could never have happened in reality. He had never given it any practical thought, not like he was giving this.

Now that he had time and distance from the whole experience, he could see that he had admired Lady Ann in much the same way a courtly love poet would admire his lady love from afar. It hadn't been real. It hadn't burned him from the inside the way thoughts of Bronwen did.

He always admired honesty, even when he was telling himself a hard truth. He wanted Bronwen for his own. He could see their future, imagine a life stretching out in front of them, one full of conversations and quiet moments. That he did not feel he was good enough for her didn't stop the yearning. The very thought of her wedded to another man burned his soul, and yet what choice did he have?

If he had never seen Ioan and his room, he would have no evidence of any wrongdoing and could perhaps contemplate winning the competition. But he had, and there was no other way forward for him. The whole thing was a mess, and yet in the centre of it all was Bronwen, shining like a jewel, a jewel he desperately wanted but knew he had no right to even attempt to take.

He pushed himself away from the wall. Gazing up at Bronwen's window like a lovesick fool was helping no one. He was not going to go to her, so he should stalk the shadows of the castle and hunt for more evidence of what was going on here.

He moved softly away, looking and listening for anything that might help his mission. But as he walked, even as he told himself not to, he couldn't help but compose a poem about the way one woman made him feel.

Chapter Nineteen

Bronwen knew she was a coward. She'd issued the last challenge of the competition yesterday evening and then fled to her chamber before Hugh could speak to her. Not that he'd made a move to come towards her, but she needed time to think, time when she wasn't looking at him.

It hadn't helped.

Now, here she was, the Great Hall full of people waiting to hear the knights' poems, and she'd still not made a decision about her future.

Should she follow her plan, to marry a man who didn't make her feel? A man who would not have the power to hurt her, a man who would provide a calm, if boring life. She wanted boring, wanted the stability of knowing what to expect from the man she married, or so she'd always believed.

Sir John fulfilled her requirements. He seemed like a pleasant, competent man. She could see her life with him. It would be peaceful. He would never have a hold over her. If he made snide remarks about her appearance or her personality, it might sting but it would not take away who she was as a person. She would not become her mother.

But it wasn't what she wanted, not deep down, not if she was really honest with herself. She wanted the fire and passion that Hugh ignited in her. She wanted his twinkling eyes and his sure-footed capabilities. She wanted a man who couldn't lie and who defended others who were not as strong as him.

Now her decision was down to what she always believed she wanted and what she wanted right now in this moment. She had no idea which way she was going to go.

A gong sounded and the hall slowly quietened.

Her father, wearing a heavily embroidered red cloak, sailed towards the dais. This was a mood she recognised well. He was playing the benevolent lord, the man who would bestow favours on his underlings. It meant he was sober, which was normally something to be rejoiced, but tonight might not work in her favour.

She wanted her father not to remember too clearly the winner of the tournament being announced. If he woke the following morning and didn't remember how the winner was chosen, she would easily be able to convince him that it had been his decision. She would have to hope that the poems would turn him to drink, an awful thing to say and normally something she would avoid, but this time it was her life that was hanging in the balance. Her whole plan had hinged on his lack of sobriety.

'Welcome, knights, gentlewomen, one and all. We are gathered here this evening to listen to the finest art of being a knight, the composition of courtly love poetry,' her father announced.

A murmur of appreciation circled the hall. There was only room for her father on the dais. Perhaps she should go up and stand next to him, but she couldn't force her feet to move. This decision was so important, so life-altering that the sheer enormity of it was like a weight pressing her down, keeping her feet rooted to the floor beneath.

Someone brushed against her arm and goose bumps erupted along her skin.

'I don't have to do this,' a deep voice sounded in her ear.

She knew what Hugh meant, but she wasn't ready to address it. 'Are you that sure your poem will win?' Despite the seriousness of the situation, her lips twitched as she teased him.

'It is undoubtedly a masterpiece of perfection, like everything I do.'

She couldn't stop the smile that spread across her face. 'I'm sure it is.'

'But I...'

Whatever Hugh had been about to say was drowned out by the first knight stepping forward to read out his poem. Bronwen was glad, because if Hugh had been about to suggest that he not read out his composition, she wouldn't have known what to have told him. It was still too soon and...she knew that was foolish, that she would have to make up her mind in mere moments, but she still needed time to think.

The first knight approached her father and began to speak. Bronwen had to bite her lips to stop herself from laughing out loud. The poem, clearly meant to describe her, wasn't bad. It wasn't fabulous either, but it passed muster and wouldn't have amused her normally if it wasn't for the situation. Instead of addressing her, the subject of the poem, the knight had chosen to face her father and speak the words to him. There was something absurd about the young man addressing her father's solemn face.

Next to her, Hugh's shoulders shook silently, and it took all her will power not to giggle. She wouldn't humiliate a man by doing that to him as he spoke his words, but the effort was Herculean.

Mercifully, the poem came to an end and the knight stepped back. Bronwen clapped to show her appreciation, and the crowd joined in, some calling out praise and encouragement. The knight took his place back in the crowd, a pleased smile on his face, his friends slapping him on the back.

'This tournament has been good for that,' said Hugh.

'Good for what?' she asked, still not turning to look at him. If she didn't see him, she might still be able to think clearly.

'It's built good friendships among some of the men. It will hold them in good stead when they work together on the battlefield.'

'And you, have you made friends?' Somehow that was important to her.

There was a pause and then, 'Yes, I believe I have.'

Before she could question him more, another knight pushed to the fore. From the grins of the spectators, this was going to be good. And it was. It wasn't vaguely romantic, but it was very amusing, and the mood in the hall shifted, the solemnity dropped from her father's face, and he called for ale before gesturing for her to come and stand by his side. She was reluctant to step away from Hugh but knew that she must.

The readings sped up after that. With the ale flowing freely, the mood went from solemn to jovial for everyone else but her. Neither Sir John nor Sir Hugh had spoken their verses, and her whole body was trembling with anticipation.

She still had no idea whom she was going to crown the winner. It wouldn't be any of the men who had spoken so far. Their poems may have been the best ever spoken, but she couldn't hear them. Sir John spoke his, his gaze flicking to her every now and again, a soft smile in his eyes. He was a good man and would make a decent husband. If she picked him, she was almost sure she could persuade her father that he was the best match, especially if he'd had enough ale. Judging by the colour of his face, that moment was soon upon them.

Sir Gwilliam stepped up. Without thinking, she turned to her father. 'Why is he still here?'

Her father waved his tankard around. 'He's from a wealthy family, he'd be a good ally.'

Her heart dropped. 'But he's a horrid person.' Being married to a man who took glory in hurting others, who would stab a man when his back was turned, was worse than remaining at Ceinwen Castle. She would rather die than be subjected to a moment alone with such a man. 'I cannot marry him.'

Lord Geraint shrugged. 'I am wedded to a shrew.' Bronwen wanted to tear her father's eyes out for his casual dismissal of her mother. She was not how her father described. She was loving and devoted and vulnerable to the way she had been treated. 'We don't get to choose who we marry,' her father continued. 'That's for our parents to decide. I am still considering Sir Gwilliam to be your husband, and you will abide by my choice.'

'But...' In all of her plans, she had not truly believed her father would be competent enough to make a judgement when the time came.

He glowered up at her, his eyes narrowed, his skin splotchy with red patches, which seemed to protrude and pulse. 'You do not get to comment.'

Bronwen's blood ran cold. This was her father at his worst: drunk and belligerent. And it had to happen on the evening her future was being decided.

While they had been talking, Sir Gwilliam had waited, but now that they had fallen silent he began. Bronwen couldn't even say that his poem was bad. Despite his near constant smirk, Sir Gwilliam had a rich baritone which served his words well. The hall stilled as everyone began to listen to him, and a sick feeling of dread curled in her stomach. He could not win this, he could not.

She turned away from Sir Gwilliam, searching the hall for her father's closest cronies, hoping that they would distract him, but unusually, she could not see them among the faces of those crowded into the hall, and when she turned back to the spot where Hugh had been standing, he had gone too.

She couldn't get the air into her lungs, it was as if a huge weight pressed down on her, restricting her breathing.

She needed her father's cronies to distract him, and she needed Hugh because... She didn't know how to put a name to the swirling emotions inside her, only that somehow Hugh had become her anchor, the man she needed to see when everything seemed so uncertain.

Sir Gwilliam droned on. It must have been good, because maidens and matrons were sighing, one even dabbed her eyes.

Bronwen heard none of it.

The words stretched into eternity. Next to her, her father was nodding along.

Snakes curled in her stomach.

After an age, the poem finally came to an end. It was too soon.

There was still no sign of Hugh.

Her father stood. Everything seemed to be happening in slow motion.

'As that's everyone...'

'No!' The hall went deathly silent at her outburst. She had never openly contradicted her father before.

'That is to say,' she said, softening her tone. 'Sir Hugh has not given us his poem yet.'

The current choice was between Sir Gwilliam and Sir John. Sir John was the sensible decision, and yet she couldn't make it, not yet, and if her father made the choice for her, well, he was not going to choose Sir John because the man was not good enough in his eyes. If Hugh didn't recite his poem, then Sir Gwilliam would win the tournament, and that would mean... Bronwen couldn't finish that thought, it would bring her to her knees.

'Sir Hugh,' her father called out. 'Are you ready to impress us with your composition?' There was a resounding silence; Bronwen forgot how to breathe. 'It appears he doesn't want to tell us his.'

A titter of amused laughter circled the hall led by Sir Gwilliam. Bronwen didn't know how she was still standing; her legs were no longer steady. She could not marry Sir Gwilliam, she could not. He was cruel and...and he was not Hugh. Hugh, who she had thought cared enough to want to enter this final contest and who appeared to have walked away right at the crucial moment. She pressed a hand to her chest. Underneath her palm, her heart splintered into a thousand pieces.

'If that is it, then we need to announce the tournament winner.' Ale sloshed over the rim of her father's tankard as he waved his arm around.

Sir Gwilliam smirked at her and her blood turned to ice. Living with him would be worse than with her father, she would not care for her husband, but that did not mean he would not be able to destroy her. His cruelty would eat away at her until she was nothing more than a shadow.

Even though she knew it was pointless, her gaze roamed the hall, searching for a sign that Hugh was there, that he was going to rescue her after all. But he was not to be found; he had forsaken her.

Her heartbeat pounded in her ears; her breathing ragged. She could barely hear her father as he continued to talk. She hadn't truly believed Hugh when he had said he would not try to win the competition, had thought that something had happened between them, something special that would make him at least try…but she had given him no encouragement, no indication that she might consider him, hadn't even realised until this moment that *he* was the only person she wanted to consider, and so she really only had herself to blame.

And then Hugh was stepping into the space before her father. Bronwen reached out and grasped the back of her father's chair, her fingers biting into the smooth wood. It was the only way she could keep standing.

'Forgive me,' Hugh said quietly but firmly. 'I stepped outside for a moment. If I am not too late, I would like to present my poem.'

Bronwen's knees shook violently. Hugh had come, he hadn't abandoned her. His gaze locked with hers and something shot between them, something hot and potent, something that pulled her back to all their shared moments, the breathless kissing, the laughter and the way he looked at her as if he truly saw her for who she was. She wanted to tell him how grateful she was that he had returned to her in this moment, that he had not forsaken her when she needed him the most, but even if they hadn't had an audience, she would not have been able to find the words to express all that she was feeling.

He began his poem. His words flowed over her, the cadence of his voice holding her captive. At first, she did not hear what he said, the relief that she had another option to choose flooding through her so strong it drowned almost everything else out. Slowly, inexorably, she was drawn into his words, their gaze held, and she wanted to cross the space dividing them and lean in so that only she could hear what he was saying.

'The warmth of her eyes on a summer's day…'

As she listened, she realised he was talking about her, really truly her, and not the person all the other knights had described. None of the other men really knew her, not like this…

'The leaves rustle in the tress above but all I see is her smile.'

And now he was talking about their time in the woods together, when he had kept her safe, and the words he spoke were full of passion and desire, and some other emotion laced through it. Something was happening to her chest, something painful and sweet and unidentifiable. For the first time in her life, she felt truly seen.

The rest of the hall was silent and still as Hugh spoke, his words coursing through her veins. She couldn't have torn her gaze away from him for all the wealth of the kingdom. He finished, there was a beat of silence, and then the room burst into cheers.

For a long while, they stayed staring at one another, the moment stretching between them, the air between them shimmering with unspoken words.

Somebody slapped him on the back, jolting him and breaking their connection. Bronwen inhaled a deep breath before leaning down and speaking to her father. 'You said you did not mind whether I married Sir Gwilliam or Sir Hugh.'

His anger from earlier had mellowed, the redness of his skin had faded, and his eyes had taken on the glazed look he wore when the ale began to dim his responses. This was what she had hoped for all along, only she'd wanted more options, to be able to choose someone who would incite nothing from her, not fear and certainly not desire.

'Both men would make good allies,' he said, leaning to the left more than was necessary.

'I think it would be more dramatic if I made the announcement.' It would be taking the limelight away from her father, and she was not sure whether he'd had enough to drink for that. He did love to be the centre of attention.

Fortunately, he'd now reached that level of drunkenness that normally indicated the start of his generous mood and less of an inclination to move from wherever he was seated. 'Yes, you announce it.' Before she could straighten, he grasped her arm. 'Do not make a fool of me.'

He let go of her before she could question how she could.

All eyes were on her. Hugh with his usual calm expression, Sir Gwilliam with his habitual sneer and Sir John with his compassion and hope and all the other knights and members of her father's household ranging behind them. She wished she could have a moment, only a brief pause, so that she could thank Hugh for stepping forward, for giving her options when all had seemed lost, but all eyes were on her and she had nowhere to go.

'My family and I are deeply honoured by the presence at our tournament by each and every one of you,' she began. 'We do hope that you have enjoyed your time here, as much as we have delighted in having you stay with us.'

A cheer went up from everybody, and she tucked her fingers into the folds of her skirts so that no one would see how much she was shaking.

'Lord Geraint and I have been impressed with all your courage and skills.' Behind her, her father snorted, and she hoped it was only her who heard the derisive noise. She said some more words still, for some unfathomable reason not able to say whom she had chosen, but then there was no real choice. There hadn't been ever since she had seen Sir Hugh that first day in the woods, no matter how much she had told herself to be logical. She had wanted to protect her heart, but that had been a pointless endeavour. Her mouth was dry, and the tips of her fingers were icy cold, but she knew what she had to say.

Hugh gazed up at the raised platform, a strange stillness creeping over him. After all that he'd done, all that he'd risked, was Bronwen going to choose to marry Gwilliam after all? Surely not; the man was a thing from nightmares. Bronwen must know that even though Hugh was not perfect, he was a better choice than Gwilliam. Hugh would always treat her with the respect she deserved, she would never experience the level of cruelty her father showed to her mother, and given time, he could make her care for him as strongly as he cared for her.

And yet…it would be better if she chose Gwilliam. Hugh was going to have to reveal to the higher-ups at Windsor what he had just learned in the courtyard as soon as he could. He should not even be in the hall right now. Once he'd learned who was behind the treasonous plot, he should have jumped on Guardo and ridden away as fast as the stallion could move, but he hadn't headed towards the stables, hadn't even given it a thought. Instead, his legs had carried him into the hall, towards her, the only person who had the power to stop him doing his duty.

The poems had appeared to be over. Bronwen's eyes were tight as her gaze searched the hall. He'd fancied she was looking for him, waiting to hear what he had to say, and even though he knew he should not, he could not help himself but push forward and offer his poem. But as her speech continued without announcing the winner, he began to wonder if the look in her eyes had been a trick of the light or his own longing reflected back at him.

Sweat began to bead across his brow, but he resisted the urge to wipe it away. He would not fidget, no one here would know what it would do to him if Bronwen did not chose him as the winner of the tournament. He would appear to face the rejection as he always did, with calmness and acceptance, and then he would leave, because it would intolerable to be around her for a moment longer.

Bronwen paused. The silence was palpable.

Hugh stilled; he wasn't even sure he was breathing.

And then, Bronwen spoke. 'I am very pleased to announce that Sir Hugh is the winner.'

Chapter Twenty

Hugh stood at one end of the Great Hall, sweat coating his back, his clothes sticking to his skin. He scrubbed a hand down his face. *This would be fine.* Because it had to be. Every decision he'd made, every action he'd followed had been done with the very best of intentions. But even so, waiting for his bride to arrive was unexpected.

He inhaled, embarrassed that the sound was shuddery and glad there was no one close to him to be aware of it. He wanted Bronwen, wanted her with a ferocity that took his breath away. And he was getting her. From this moment forward, she would be his. No matter what the future held. Part of him was wary; he'd not told her the truth, and his actions differed wildly from his plan. But for the most part, he was triumphant, exhilarated in a way he had never experienced before.

A crowd was gathering behind him, although it

was smaller than the one from last night when his victory had been announced. Several of the knights had already left, on to the next tournament neither bitter nor surprised that Hugh had won. Sir Gwilliam had left in a rage, threatening dire consequences for Hugh, which were unlikely to ever come to pass. The man might have a cruel streak, but he was a bully and would find someone else to put down within the week. Sir John had left quietly without a word to anyone. Hugh would have felt bad about dashing the man's hopes if he hadn't had so many other things to think about.

A priest came to stand before him, and something began to claw its way out of Hugh's chest, its progress painful and slow. In only a few moments, Bronwen would arrive, and they would bind their lives together until death parted them, and he had a secret that could destroy them both before they had even begun.

The priest said a few words to him, but he had no idea what. He nodded because he thought that's what the man wanted, but the priest may have requested Hugh stand on his head and he'd be none the wiser.

Despite everything he knew, despite the fact that Bronwen had only chosen him because he was not Gwilliam and not because she specifically wanted Hugh, he had wanted her for himself, and selfishly, he had taken her. Guilt burned within him. By marrying her, he may have saved her from Gwilliam, but that did not change the fact that he had nowhere for her to live once they were married, one of her biggest desires in finding a husband. He did not even know how he would go about finding somewhere. No matter how the anxiety clawed at him, it was not strong enough for him to reverse his decision. He would marry Bronwen and face the consequences, whatever they might be, because he had never wanted anyone or anything more than he wanted to be with her.

The babble of voices around him quietened and he knew, without turning, that Bronwen was standing at the entrance.

He turned slowly, his breath catching in his throat as he laid eyes on his bride. There she was, so beautiful and so full of goodness that only he seemed to truly know about. The anxious clawing beast inside of him stilled as his whole being centred on her.

This was the right thing to do.

Whatever happened next, he was sure of that. Even when she realised what a bad bargain she had made, he was glad of what he had done because it meant that, for better or for worse, Bronwen was going to be his.

Bronwen deserved better than living here with a neglectful father, surrounded by dishonest men and hangers-on. And, yes, he may not have been entirely honest with her about why he was here, but he was sure she would understand the reason why once he was in a position to explain. He had to believe that.

Their gazes locked, and she began to move towards him. He *would* take care of her, and he would protect her mother too, if that's what she wanted. Bronwen would never have cause to be uncertain about her future again. She would know peace and security, even if it cost him his soul.

She came to a stop in front of him. Her eyes were wide, her skin pale, and he smiled, trying to show her all the reassurance he could with the simple gesture. This marriage wasn't what she wanted. She'd wanted a man who could provide a stable home for her, and he could not do that, but it was what she had chosen, and maybe she had made that choice because it was either him or a man who thought cruelty was natural, but Hugh would do everything to ensure she never felt it was the wrong decision.

The priest began to talk, addressing them and those who had come to witness the ceremony. She was standing so close to him he could see the pulse in her neck; it was fluttering so fast, like a bird in a trap. Her chest was rising and falling quickly. He touched the back of his hand to hers. It was meant to offer her comfort, but she was so cold that he laced his fingers with hers, rubbing the back of them with his thumb to try and get some warmth into her skin.

'All will be well,' he murmured as the ceremony carried on around them.

The eyes that gazed back at him told him she was not so sure. She was right to worry. In this moment, he had no idea what their future would hold, only that he would do everything he could to make her happy.

He tightened his grip on her fingers and she squeezed back. The tip of her tongue wetted her top lip, and he fought to hold himself still as other needs, far more primal, crashed over him.

'I'm afraid,' she murmured.

'I will never hurt you.'

She stared up at him for an endless moment as if she were looking into his soul. Eventually, she blinked and turned her attention to his chest. He was not sure whether she'd believed him. Hell, he knew he wouldn't if he were in her position.

'You could,' she said so quietly he had to lean down to hear her. Her gaze flickered up to his again, and her expression was like a dagger to the chest. 'You could hurt me more than anyone.'

Everything inside him stilled. Did she know what he had discovered last night? But, no, that would be impossible. She had been listening to the poems when he'd realised so many of her father's closest comrades were not in the hall. It was nothing to slip out unnoticed by all, with everyone so rapt on the drama happening within its walls that no one had noticed his exit. The men he was looking for were so complacent, so used to not getting caught, it had not been hard to find them. They'd gathered in the stables and talked through their plans for the next few weeks. Hugh had stood in open-mouthed shock at what they had discussed so openly and without fear of recrimination. He had everything that he needed. His mission was a success. He had found the traitors. Is this what she meant by hurting her? He would try his very best to make sure that the consequences from his discovery did not impact her.

'I vow to you…' he began.

She shook her head slightly. 'Don't bind yourself into a promise you may not be able to keep.'

'I *will* take care of you.'

'I know you will.'

'I *will* protect you.'

Hadn't he already proven that? He could have left Ceinwen Castle the moment he had discovered the truth last night. He had almost done it; he'd thought about waiting for the men to finish their discussion and then grabbing his horse and riding to Tristan to tell him all that he had discovered. From there he would have travelled on to Windsor to inform Sir

Benedictus, the man running the country in the king's absence, of the plans. That is what he should have done. That is what the logical side of his mind, the one he had always followed until now, had all but yelled at him to do. He hadn't.

He'd been certain that Lady Bronwen would choose Sir John as her husband. The man was steady, had his own home and appeared to be kind. Hugh had been... fine with that, he had decided. Although his actions had proven his belief a lie.

Yes, she had chosen him first, but it was only because the alternative was worse, and for some reason, Sir John had not been in the picture. Someone had mentioned to him that Sir John's poem had not been good. It had taken away some of his joy at winning, but it had not dampened his enthusiasm to make Bronwen his.

The long-winded ceremony finally came to an end, and they were pronounced husband and wife. He couldn't stop the smile that spread across his face, which only got wider as Bronwen's own face broke into the same expression, her hazel eyes shining up at him.

She would forgive him, he decided. When he finally told her about his mission, she would understand why he'd had to keep the truth of it from her. And when it came to finding her somewhere to live while he was off on campaign, he would make sure that it was somewhere not only safe but somewhere she could be happy.

He may not have been the husband she would have chosen if she'd had more of a say, but that did not mean their marriage would be a disaster. He would do everything in his power to make her life with him a good one.

They would make this marriage work; they had to. The alternative did not bear thinking about.

Chapter Twenty-One

Someone had lit a fire in Bronwen's chamber even though it had been a warm day. She was glad for it because she could not stop trembling, although she was not cold as such. Everything had happened so quickly. One moment, she had been facing the prospect of tying herself to Sir Gwilliam for the rest of her life, and the next she had chosen Hugh, and the warmth and relief that had flooded through her had been as unexpected as the joy that followed.

But there had been no time to talk to him. Her father had whisked him away and had spent the rest of the evening in deep discussion with him, although what they had talked about, she couldn't even fathom a guess. They were as different as a golden eagle and a stone.

Today, at the ceremony, there had been no time to talk either and now she was waiting for her husband in her chamber and she had no idea what to say to him. She had repeatedly told him she was not going to let him win the tournament, but when it had come down to it, she had chosen him over all the other entrants. She had to assume he was going to ask why she had changed her mind, but to answer him would be to confront thoughts and feelings she was not ready to address, even to herself. She'd had no choice, not really. The other path was a lifetime married to Sir Gwilliam, and he was not someone she could tolerate for a few moments, let alone the rest of her mortal life. But that wasn't the whole truth.

When she had thought Hugh was not going to read his poem, the bottom had dropped out of her world in a way that had nothing to do with marrying Sir Gwilliam and everything to do with Hugh. She didn't want to think about it, didn't want to acknowledge that, after all her protestations, she had not followed her practical side after all and had instead given into her cravings to be with a man she desired above all others. She had to hope that she would not, after everything she had always planned for, turn into her mother, that Hugh would continue to be kind and thoughtful and true.

She had no idea of what he expected from this union, but she knew that tonight they would consummate their vows, and that is what had her hands shaking.

She held her hand out to the flames. The warmth was soothing, but it did not stop the fine tremors that ran over her. She did not think it would be long before Hugh joined her, he seemed to find feasts as enjoyable as she did, that is to say, not much at all. She wondered whether she should undress herself or whether he would want to do that. She knew what to expect of the next part of her marriage. Her mother had told her everything, not wanting her daughter to be ignorant on her wedding night. Bronwen had seen and heard enough around the castle to know that what passed between a man and a woman could be very enjoyable for both people, and she had enjoyed the times she and Hugh kissed, more than she had thought possible. She hadn't asked her mother about that aspect. There was only so much a daughter wanted to know.

She had hopes it would be good for both Hugh and her. If their shared kisses were anything to go by, it had to be. But she couldn't imagine how they would go from fully dressed to him lying between her legs. The sheer awkwardness of getting to that point had her whole body cringing.

She half hoped, half dreaded that Hugh would know what to do. The thought of him with a woman who wasn't her made her feel sick, but then this whole situation would be worse if he had as little clue as her as to how to make this happen.

Heavy footsteps sounded outside in the corridor before coming to a stop outside her chamber door. She held her breath but, for a while, there was only silence.

It had to be Hugh, but what was he doing out there? It was unfathomable that he was as nervous as her. He was always so confident and sure, and she had assumed that he would act in the same way regarding their wedding night. She would have gone on believing that had she not felt his slight tremble when he took her hand earlier. During that whole ceremony, he had clung to her fingers as if she might disappear at any moment, which was exactly the way she had clung to him.

When he still did not open the chamber door, she made her way over to it and opened if for him.

His size filled the doorway, his lids were hooded, but his eyes burned, and she knew that he craved her as much as she did him.

She stood aside and he stepped into the room, his boots loud on the floorboards.

'Come over to the fire where it's warmer,' she said, fluttering around him as if she were a small bird trying to find somewhere to land.

He seemed impossibly large in her private space.

Or perhaps she was very small. Either way, maybe it wouldn't work between them after all.

'Do not be afraid,' he said gently as he stopped in front of the fireplace.

She swallowed; he was asking for the impossible. Her future happiness rested on him, and there was still so much uncertainty about what happened next. But she didn't voice those thoughts. She wasn't sure she would ever be able to.

They stood facing each other before the fire, the bed looming large to their right.

'How should we do this?' she asked when she could bear the tension no more.

He laughed softly. 'I have not done this before.'

'Bedded a wife?'

He swallowed hard, his fingers tightening on hers. 'Bedded anyone. You will be my first.'

Something hot and possessive curled in her stomach as her soul triumphed. 'And your last.'

An answering heat flared in his eyes. 'Your first, your last too.'

'Yes.'

He nodded, an unreadable emotion filling his gaze. And then he was kissing her as if everything depending on their mouths joining, which in some way it did.

Moments or days later, it was hard to tell, Hugh lifted his head. He must have dropped her hands at some point, because hers now threaded through his hair. His own pinned her tightly to him.

'We should stop that,' he slurred.

'Why?' she whined. If it was up to her, that is all they would ever do.

A smile touched his lips. 'Because I do not want to lose my mind and take you like a wild animal. I promised I would not hurt you, and I will treat you gently.'

She almost stamped her foot. 'That is not what I want. I like this wildness in you. It is a side others do not see.'

He let out a shuddery breath. 'Next time, you will not need so much care, but this first time...' His lips ghosted across her forehead. 'This time, we must go slowly, learn what each other likes.'

'I like you losing control,' she protested again, and he groaned softly.

'I know I have not done this before, but I have been told that it hurts a woman the first time. I do not want that for you.'

She mulled over what he was saying, her hands running over the length of his arms, tracing the curves of his muscles. 'I know the point at which it will be painful for me, but until then, there is no need to be gentle with me. I will not break.'

For a long moment, he held still. She wondered if she had shocked him. Perhaps he was hoping for a mild, docile wife in the bedchamber. But then his mouth came down on hers once more. This was no soft coaxing; it was all raw power and need. Clothes were discarded. Hands stroked and pinched and did wonderfully wicked things to parts of her body that had never been touched before. She was a mass of nerve endings teetering on the edge of something primal when he finally lifted his head, and she realised they had made it to the bed without her even noticing.

'I…you…perfect…' he managed before claiming her mouth once more.

Laughter bubbled up inside her because she couldn't have put it better herself. The hot, hard length of him brushed against her entrance, and she strained against him, desperate to feel him move inside her.

'Now?' he questioned against her neck.

'Now,' she agreed, pulling his mouth back to hers.

He surged forward, pushing into her. She gasped into his mouth as pain, quick as lightening, shot through her.

He stilled, bracing himself on his forearms. He held himself above her. 'You are all right?' Sweat beaded across his forehead, his jaw clenched as if in pain.

'Yes,' she breathed. 'I'm all right.'

He didn't move within her, but he did lower his mouth until it connected with hers once more. They began to kiss again, slowly at first, but gradually she lost herself again in the rhythm of his mouth and tongue. Her body began to relax, and the pain gradually subsided. Without thinking, she began to move beneath him, slowly at first and then with increasing desperation.

He grabbed her waist, holding her still. 'Careful.' He growled.

'Are you hurt?'

He choked out a laugh. 'No. Feels good. So good.'

'Then why…?'

'No end. Not yet.'

She frowned. She had no idea what he was talking about. There was no need for it to end; she could do this forever.

'You're not there,' he murmured. Now she was even more confused. She was right here, with him.

He reached a hand between their bodies until his fingers brushed a part of her between her legs. 'Oh,' she gasped. 'Oh, what…?'

She felt his smile against her mouth as he continued to press against her, and now he was moving again. She tried to tell him that she had never felt this way, but she could not have formed a sentence if her life depended on it. Her garbled words seemed to spur him on, and then something happened to her, something marvellous and bewildering, and the sum of everything she had ever wanted.

Afterwards, she lay gasping as all his weight collapsed on her. That had been…there were no words. She had enjoyed their kisses, had craved more of them for days, but she had never imagined something so marvellous as that would happen between them. She ran her hands down the length of his back, enjoying the ripple of muscles beneath her fingers. She was content and warm, and her bones had all turned to liquid. In this moment, everything was perfect.

She must have fallen asleep, because she woke to a warm cloth on the inside of her legs.

'There's blood,' murmured Hugh as he worked the material over her. 'I did not mean to be so rough. I…'

'It was perfect,' she told him. 'Absolutely perfect.'

'Thank goodness,' he murmured, dropping his forehead onto her chest. 'I could not bear it if I had hurt you.'

'I have never felt so good in all my life.' It was true. She was slightly tender between her legs, but it was nothing. 'I have been more sore after a day of riding,' she told him, threading her fingers through his hair. 'How was it for you?'

'Sublime,' he said simply.

'Can we do it again?'

He lifted his head. 'Now?'

'Is it too soon? Do you need to rest?'

He laughed, his whole body shaking against hers.

'No, I am ready again.' He shifted against her, and she felt the evidence of his words against her thigh. 'But are you sure you are not too uncomfortable?'

'I am positive.'

That was all the encouragement he needed for them to begin again.

Hugh stared up at the ceiling, not that he could make it out in the darkness, a huge smile plastered across his face. Next to him, his wife slept.

His wife!

He'd never expected to marry, had even half expected Bronwen to change her mind before the ceremony, but they were less than two full days into their marriage, and he knew it was the greatest decision he had ever made.

Like any man, he had thought about lovemaking a lot. From what he'd gathered from conversations and from living in such confined spaces, having seen others engaged in the act, he imagined it slightly rougher than most people. He hadn't expected to find a woman who wanted it in the same way, and when he had thought about doing it with Bronwen, and he had thought of it more times than he would care to admit, he had imagined that she would want to be treasured, and he'd been more than willing to do that, desperate even.

The night before the wedding, when he'd finally allowed his imagination to run wild, he'd hoped that he might be able to introduce some of his fantasies in a few years from now when she trusted that he wouldn't hurt her. He would never have imagined that Bronwen would want the same as him. The mild-mannered lady whose serene countenance had turned many of the knights' heads was nowhere to be found in the marriage chamber.

He'd thought taking her virginity and losing his own would be a mildly embarrassing affair. He'd wanted to make her enjoy it, but his limited experience with women had not involved the taking of virginity, and he hadn't been sure he would know instinctively where to touch her to make it an enjoyable experience for her. He'd never imagined she would be as insatiable as himself. They had barely made it out of the chamber in over a day. The whole castle would know what they were up to, but he found he didn't care.

Ioan ap Cadfael and his men could go and invade the whole country, and Hugh wouldn't mind so long as they left this chamber alone.

He brushed her hair off his face and she mumbled something incoherent, which only made him smile wider. She moved against him and his body began to harden again. He almost couldn't believe it possible. Surely, he had used his member so much that it would hurt to go again. But, no, his body was ready and willing.

''Gain?' Bronwen murmured.

'I thought you were asleep.'

'Dozing.' She brushed her thigh against him and he groaned. 'You want…again?'

He was glad it was her who was having difficulty speaking this time.

'Are you too tired?' He couldn't believe he was asking this. He must be too tired. He hadn't ever expended this much energy, not even on the training ground. But he found that, yes, he did very much want to go again.

'Very tired.'

'Then we will sleep.' He brushed her forehead with a gentle kiss.

'No… I want you.'

His heart swelled. His mind tried to remind him that wanting to lie with him was not a declaration of devotion, but his heart didn't seem to be listening.

He slipped from underneath her and kissed the nape of her neck, feathering kisses along her spine. Her back arched towards him, and he slipped an arm around her waist.

'So beautiful,' he murmured against her skin. 'So perfect.'

He nudged open her legs with his knee and settled in between them.

'This way?' she asked.

'This way,' he confirmed, slightly raising her hips.

They both moaned as he sunk into her soft warmth. Their movements were languid, almost non-existent but every bit as delicious as before, if not more so. It had to be impossible for this joining with his wife to keep feeling better every time. If it continued in this vein, he would never do anything else.

Chapter Twenty-Two

Two days after their wedding, Bronwen finally made it out of the chamber to visit her mother, who took one look at her and burst into laughter, the sound lightening Bronwen's already happy heart.

'What is so funny?' Bronwen asked when her mother's mirth had finally died down.

'I am laughing for joy, my dear. You have been so sad for so long, and now I can see true happiness in your eyes. I am so glad you chose Sir Hugh to be your husband and not Sir John.'

Bronwen started. She had no idea her mother had known she had been contemplating anyone in particular, had no idea really that her mother paid her much attention. But she perhaps had not been fair to the woman; she had seen more than Bronwen had realised.

'There is no need to look so surprised. When you have children of your own, you will know how to read them. Sir John was the safe, practical choice, and you pride yourself on your practicality. I am glad your heart won over that.'

'Oh, my heart is not involved.' Bronwen pressed a palm to her chest, sure that what she said was true. She had wanted Hugh because he made her body feel things, delightful things, and because he was kind and strong and, crucially, in that moment, he was not Sir Gwilliam. She liked him a lot, but she did not love him. She was sure of that; it was integral to her survival of the marriage that she did not develop feelings that were too strong to escape from.

'My dear, there is no shame in loving your husband. In fact, some might say it is very important that you do.'

'I am not ashamed of my feelings but...it is too soon to love him.' Bronwen did not want to tell her mother the real reason why she would never love the man to whom she had bound herself. She did not want to hurt her mother's feelings by raking over the remnants of her marriage to her father.

Her mother seemed to accept her explanation, although her amused glances suggested she did not believe her daughter's protestations. Bronwen didn't know how much time she spent with her mother; she only knew that her craving for Hugh grew as the time went past, until it was almost intolerable that she had not felt his lips on her skin in what appeared to be an entire lifetime.

She made her excuses and left, her mother's soft laughter following her down the hall. Bronwen practically bounced back to her chamber, but she stopped when she saw Hugh.

She'd left him sleeping in their bed, but he was now standing at the window gazing down at the courtyard below, every line of his body tensed for action.

'What are you doing?' she asked, a creeping sense of foreboding settling over her.

'I…' He turned back to her, and there was something in his gaze that had her stomach turning over.

'Hugh…'

'It's nothing.'

She knew, deep down, that it wasn't nothing. If it was, he'd be striding towards her and scooping her up in his arms before carrying her to the bed to carry on from where they had left off. 'Do not lie to me Hugh. You are not good at that, remember?'

He scrubbed a hand down his face. 'I… There's something I need to tell you. Something I should have mentioned before, but I…'

A hard rock was forming in her stomach. She had no idea what he was going to tell her, but from the tone of his voice, the news he was about to impart was not good.

'When I came here…' He paused, his gaze darting about the chamber, landing everywhere that was not her. 'I came here because…'

Please, she begged internally, *please let him not have an ulterior motive for being at the tournament.*

She could not take it if everything they had built together had been founded on a lie.

'I came here because…'

'You keep saying that,' she snapped.

His lips downturned, his gaze tortured. The fact that she was able to read his expressions did not make her feel better.

'There were rumours of a treasonous plot here at Ceinwen.'

'What?' Of all the things…

'Of someone acting against the king.'

'I know what treason means.' Her heart hurt, almost as if it was physically wounded. Her father might be an old sot, but he was not disloyal to the king, of that she was…fairly sure.

'Of course.'

'Who is spreading these rumours? What do they have to do with Ceinwen Castle?' She was pacing now, unable to sit still. Thoughts swirled through her mind, each one more awful than the next. 'Was my father suspected of these acts?' One look at Hugh's face confirmed her worst fears. 'You came here to investigate my father?' It was obvious now. A knight of Sir Hugh's calibre did not travel to a remote part of Wales to compete for a wife. Why would he need to?

'Yes.' The confirmation was a deep blow to her stomach; she doubled over as pain whipped through her.

Hugh reached for her, but she moved away from his touch.

She'd known that he had not travelled here for *her* specifically. She hadn't minded that. He hadn't known her before the start of the tournament, but to realise that he had been in Ceinwen for another reason altogether, that he had been investigating her family the whole time... It was a betrayal on a scale she could not begin to comprehend, worse than finding out that he was a secret drunk.

'What have you found out? Is he a traitor?'

'No.'

She held her head high, even as she wanted to crumple to the floor with relief. 'You came here to discover a traitor and instead gained a wife. What a waste of time for you.'

She waited for him to deny that becoming her husband was a waste, waited to see if they could salvage something from their relationship, but he did not. 'I did not say I had not discovered a traitor, only that I do not believe your father is involved. From what I understand, he is being used as a front. The wealth here can only be partially attributed to the fertility of the area, a large portion of the spending here must be from ill-gotten gains.'

The air rushed out of her lungs, and she gripped the edge of the table as she tried to catch her breath. 'Wh-what…?'

'Easy.' He reached out a hand to steady her, but she brushed him off.

She caught his pained swallow before he turned away. Her rejection had hurt him, and she was distraught enough to be pleased about that. All this time, she had thought they were building something, but to find out he had been using her this whole time. It was as if her heart had split into two pieces; it was remarkable that she was still standing, conversing as if her world was not ending. She'd wanted a man who was the complete opposite of her father and had found someone much worse.

'Who?' she demanded.

'Ioan ap Cadfael is the leader, I believe. I imagine he enjoys the finer things in life and is using your father as a way of getting them while he bides his time before the act of treason is committed.'

She staggered over to the bed and sank onto its edge. 'Ioan ap Cadfael,' she repeated.

'Yes.'

'But he's been here for years.' As much as she didn't like the man, she could not imagine him plotting something behind her father's back, Ioan had given every impression of being devoted to the man.

'Yes.'

The silence that followed was sharp. She had so many questions, but her distress and rage were so great, she could not think clearly. For once, she'd thought that she could trust someone, that she had found someone who was on her side, but she had been wrong. Hugh had been using her whether he had meant to or not. All this time, all these days, everything that had passed between them had been founded on a lie, and she did not know how she could go on, knowing that her husband had lied to her for the whole duration of their acquaintance.

'Why are you telling me now?' she asked.

He gestured to the bed. 'It no longer felt right to keep it from you and…'

Surely he should have thought of that before they lay together, before they had married even. There must have been some point when he had decided that lying to her was worth it. It dawned on her that he had not finished his sentence. What more could there be?

'And?' Her voice sounded strange, as if it were coming from a long way off.

'And things will come to a head soon. I would rather you were prepared.'

She sucked in a breath. Somehow the fact he was telling her for practical reasons hurt more than anything he had said so far. If he had told her he could no longer keep from telling her because of his feelings for her, the betrayal might not cut so deep.

'Tell me everything.'

He turned back to her but said nothing.

'Do you think I will reveal why you are here to my father?' She hated the shrillness she could hear in her voice, but really…he was the one who could not be trusted, not her.

'I don't know you well enough to judge.'

Her fingers trembled on her lap, his words cutting her once more. How much more could she take before she broke completely? Before this moment, she had thought he knew her better than anyone else ever had. 'You know I have no loyalty to my father or the men who surround him. They have been nothing but cruel and thoughtless towards my mother and me for years.'

'Have they ever hurt you?' She didn't miss the way he growled the question, but he had no right to feel cross on her behalf.

'Never as badly as this.'

He recoiled as if she had hit him. Perhaps she should feel bad about that, but she was nearly glad.

She had thought Hugh had been developing feelings for her, that he had wanted to marry her, but she had been a means to an end, a way to get closer to her father to discover what was going on at Ceinwen Castle. Their marriage had been because of what was happening, not in spite of it. He had used her, and she was not sure she would ever recover from his betrayal.

His frown cut an angry V between his thick brows. 'I have done nothing wrong.'

'Aside from keep the truth from me. You have treated me with the same contempt my father does my mother.'

He snorted. 'It is hardly the same.'

'No, it is worse.'

To think that only this morning, she had gazed at him while he slept, thinking that she could perhaps reveal that he had been her choice for her husband from the moment she had seen him and that she was so glad they had married. For the first time in her life, she had not felt alone. She would never tell him that now, never reveal that part of herself, not when getting close to her had been part of a mission. She would never allow him to know the hold he had over her.

She could see the pain in his eyes, but it did not engender her sympathy. If he was hurting, it was nothing in comparison to her.

'Who else has been committing treason in my father's castle? It cannot be Ioan by himself.'

Still he did not answer her. He did not trust her. While she had been congratulating herself on finding an ally, he was determined to keep secrets from her. She had thought her marriage might be better than her parents', but now she realised it was worse. At least her mother knew that her father was a horrible person. Bronwen was shocked into disbelief that Hugh had turned out to be completely disingenuous. She had been a fool who had abandoned her logical side as soon as she had found someone she desired. She would be paying for that mistake for the rest of her life. Still, she pressed him.

'I give you my word that I shall keep my own counsel. Nobody will hear it from me.'

He let out a long sigh and then lowered himself to the end of the bed, near her but not touching. The distance between them may have been a mile long.

'It cannot surprise you that the men who cosy up to your father are also involved. They have all been using this place to store weapons and coin, enough to equip and pay for an army.'

Even though she was braced for the news, she was still shocked. 'How do you know for sure?'

'I overheard them discussing their plans in detail.

It's fortunately how I also know your father is not privy to their plans.

'And the coin and weaponry?'

'I've seen it.'

'Where?'

'There's a storeroom not far from where Sir Wallace is recuperating.'

Her mind whirled. She knew weapons were stored in the barracks, but that was nowhere near the area of the castle to which Hugh was referring.

She stood abruptly. 'You must take me to them.'

He stood too, looming over her. 'No.'

'I shall find them for myself then.' She spun as if heading for the door, but he caught her wrist before she could take a step. His grip wasn't tight, she could move away from him if she really tried, but his touch held her still.

'It's too dangerous. These men have risked a lot to assemble the weapons and money. If they see you anywhere near them, who's to say what they will do with you?'

'What do you mean by that?'

'A traitor has no morals, no remorse. They will kill you and not worry about the consequences.'

'My father—'

'Your father has allowed this to happen. He may not have anything to do with the treasonous plot but, it is happening on his land in front of his face. Those men have taken his love for fine things, good food and plentiful ale and manipulated him as easily as if he were a child. If he has not noticed something of that magnitude, do you really think he will catch the men who kill you?'

Anger, hot and molten, flooded through her. 'How well you have assessed my family. My father would be too dull to notice the death of his only daughter. We are too ridiculous to have expected our friends to betray us and too witless to realise our husband was playing us for a fool.' Fine, so the last one was all her fault, but she was too enraged to speak properly.

He shook his head. 'I never had any intention of becoming your husband.' She gasped as his words cut like a knife. 'But—'

She held up a hand to stop him. 'You've already said enough.'

'Very well. I can see you are in no mood to be reasoned with.' His eyes glinted, his jaw tight.

She had never seen her husband like this. He was always so calm and in control. Now he looked as if he could tear down castles with his bare hands. He was a stranger in almost every sense of the word, although now she knew what it was like to run her fingers through his silken hair and that it made him growl when she raked her fingernails along the base of his spine.

She spun away from him, the sight of him almost too much for her to bear. Standing at her window, watching the courtyard below, did little to calm her nerves. How many of the people down there knew something was going on? Were they all involved? Or did they just think her ignorant, like her husband did? She'd thought they pitied her because of the actions of her father, but now she wondered if those glances had been because they had known her family was being used as a front for a treasonous plot.

Years ago, she'd believed her father's actions had killed any love between them, but now her heart hurt at the thought of a man who believed himself to be the king of his castle but was really only the jester. She closed her eyes against the view; she needed to think rationally. It was hard with the fury that was rolling through her, blackening her vision and turning her blood molten, but she needed to do it for the sake of her family's future.

'Will my father hang?' she asked softly.

Hugh cleared his throat. 'I don't know.'

Well, at least *that* was an honest response.

'He hasn't done anything wrong.' Except be a fool, but she had known that about him anyway. And really, was she any better? She had not liked the men who ate at her father's table, but she had not noticed they were plotting against the king. She had been so blinded by her own plight that she had not paid attention to what was in front of her.

'It is not my decision. I would argue that he has not committed any crime, but it will depend on who listens to what I have to say. If it is someone rational, then he might live.'

'And what will become of my family? My eldest brother thinks to inherit this castle one day, but it will be some time before he returns home. What will become of my mother in the meantime? What will become of me?'

'You are my wife.'

She snorted.

'You are my wife,' he repeated. 'Your place is by my side.'

'Don't tell me you are content to remain married into a traitorous family.'

'It doesn't matter what I want. It is done and it cannot be undone.'

Those were not the words she wanted to hear. She wanted him to tell her that he was bound to her now, that the connection between them was more than words, that it was something that existed deep down between them. She waited, but he said nothing more. She hadn't thought it possible for her heart to break any further, but she was wrong. His words rang around the chamber, slicing into her again and again.

'We will take your mother with us when we leave.'

She whirled around at that. 'We'll do what?'

'Your mother will not have to stay here. Your brothers will no doubt be informed as to what has happened, and it will be up to the king to decide what becomes of the castle.'

'We cannot just leave.' She ignored the fact that leaving is all she had wanted to do for years. 'The people will need us. A castle does not run itself.'

His face was shuttered; it was impossible to know what he was thinking. To think she had believed him when he told her he did not know how to lie. He was a master at it.

'I must leave within the next two weeks at the most, sooner if I cannot come up with a way to stop the treason myself. You are my wife and will come with me. That is the end of the discussion.'

He made as if to exit the chamber, but she had not finished with him. 'You'll have to tell my father.'

His response was immediate. 'No.'

'Why not?'

'Do you really wish me to go into detail? You know the sort of man he is.'

She crossed her arms. 'Yes, I want you to go into detail.'

His jaw clenched. 'Very well. You are forcing me to be blunt. The man spends most of his day not being able to see his own toes. He cannot be trusted with something of this importance.'

Somewhere deep inside her, Bronwen knew the truth of what he was saying, but she was too deep in her fury to allow him to be right. 'This is *his* castle. He should know, it's the right thing to do.'

'You gave me your word that you would tell no one.'

'And I won't, but you should.'

Hugh was already shaking his head. 'What will he do with that knowledge? No, let me answer that for you. He will bluster, accuse me of lying and go straight to his cronies with my accusations. That will tip them off, and it will be my dead body dumped into the river. They'll probably have you killed for good measure because they'll never be sure whether you know the truth or not. So, forgive me when I say your father is the last man on earth I would trust with this information.'

'If you play my father right, he can be your ally.'

Hugh snorted.

'He looks up to you.'

'That's only because he is always sitting down.'

'That's not what I meant, and you know it. He thinks you are an excellent knight from a respectable family. If you get the wording right and tell it to him at a good time of day, he will listen to you.'

Something in Hugh's defensive stance softened. 'When would be the right time to discuss it with him?'

'Right after he has finished his morning mass. He is at his most pious and thoughtful in those few moments after the priest has spoken with him and he has not yet had anything to drink.'

'And what are the correct words, do you think?'

'Appeal to his vanity. That is how anyone gets anything done around here.'

Hugh rubbed his chin. 'Very well, I will think on it. In the meantime, you will stick to your vow and not reveal this to anyone.'

He did not wait to see whether she agreed to his pronouncement before storming from the chamber. Bronwen crossed to the door, listening until his footsteps had faded before sinking to the floor.

Tears streamed from her eyes, but she made no effort to wipe them away. She had longed for a husband, for a man whom she could trust but about whom she did not care enough so that he would never have the power to hurt her. Instead, she had followed what her heart had told her—no, not her heart, her desire. She had sacrificed everything she had ever thought about herself all because a man kissed her. A man who was only using her to get to her father. She was worse than a fool.

Well, no longer. She would shut down the part of her that cared about Hugh. She would honour the vow she had made before God. Hugh was her husband, and she had promised to obey him, but that was as far as it would go. Her feelings for him would stop from this day forth. She would be married to him in name only. She had finally learned the lesson she should have understood years ago. The only person she could truly trust was herself.

Chapter Twenty-Three

Hugh stormed from the castle, his wife's fury echoing in his ears. She had no right to be so angry with him. He had been doing his duty, had been following plans that had been years in the making. And when she had needed him, he had been there for her. If not for him, she would be married to Sir Gwilliam, and then where would she be? Miserable and desperate, that's where!

To think he had thought himself happy. Over the last two days he'd let himself believe he had found the place he was meant to be, the person whom he was meant to be with. He'd been foolish in the extreme, and now he was going to pay for relaxing his guard.

He rounded a corner and ran smack into Ioan ap Cadfael, the impact jarring his ribs. He stepped back, his hands trembling with the effort of not ripping the man's head from his shoulders. It was him who had brought the attention of the crown to Bronwen's family, it was because of him that the rot had begun to set in, and it was because of him that Bronwen was now angry with Hugh. As a slow sneer crossed Ioan's face, Hugh curled his hands into tight fists.

'Trouble in paradise already?' Ioan sneered.

'No,' Hugh snapped.

But the man only laughed. 'The family's not difficult to manage. Keep them sated and they will do as you please. With Lord Geraint, that's food and drink. With Lady Bronwen—' Ioan laughed louder, the sound not a happy one '—we all know what she wants. She's been panting over you since you got here. Keep her happy between the sheets and your life will be an easy one.'

It was tempting to ram his fist into the man's stomach, but with monumental effort, Hugh held back. Ioan would hang soon enough and Hugh would be there to watch. He was not normally a bloodthirsty man, but in this case, he would make an exception. Instead of hitting Ioan, Hugh strode past him to the stables, the man's snide laughter echoing in his ears. Hugh would win in the end, but it was hard to keep going, keep walking away when he could so easily make Ioan regret ever speaking about Bronwen like that.

The stables were warm and sweet-smelling, but the familiar scents did nothing to soothe Hugh's fury.

Guardo snickered in greeting, and Hugh smoothed his hand over his stallion's long nose.

'I thought she might be coming to care for me,' he murmured. Guardo tossed his head. 'Ah, I see you already knew I was foolish to think so. She did choose me, you know.' Guardo bumped his head against Hugh's shoulder. 'Yes, you're right. She didn't have much of a choice, but still…that has to count for something. She's not like Lady Ann. I won't have to worry about her loyalty. She will not run off with another man as soon as I turn my back. That is not her way.' Guardo shifted his weight before settling his head against Hugh's again. 'It doesn't matter how she feels about me or me about her. We are married, and will have to make the best of it, come what may.'

Even as he said it, Hugh wasn't sure he believed his own words. Could he really live in a world where his wife could not forgive him for not telling her why he was in Ceinwen sooner, where her soft smile was no longer directed at him.

Hugh patted Guardo and let himself into the stall with his horse. He began to saddle him up, hoping that the repetitive job would soothe the edges of his fury. He would ride for as long as it took to calm down, and he would devise a plan because heaven knew he needed one desperately. He had no idea how long it would be until the men made a move against the king, so he needed to act fast, but he had no reinforcements until Leo arrived. He could hardly arrest six men and take control of the castle by himself. He was good, but not that good; no one was.

Leo should be here any day now, his task had been to escort a young maiden to her new home, hardly an onerous mission and one he should have completed by now, but Hugh needed a plan in case he hadn't. Lord knows, he could not depend on his wife to help him.

The ride did not help. By the time Hugh returned to the castle, the sun had set, but his mood had darkened even further. His anger at his wife had increased tenfold. She was his wife, and she should have supported him despite the unfortunate circumstances. He knew how she felt about her father, and yet her first instinct had been to protect him and not Hugh. Did that mean she wanted to cover up the traitorous plot? He'd been too emotional earlier to stop and question her, but the ride had brought that pivotal question to the forefront of his mind.

He stalked to their chamber and flung open the door.

Bronwen was standing at the foot of the bed in almost the exact same position he had left her.

He strode over to her, intending to say everything he had thought of during the long afternoon riding, but before he could speak, her arms came around his neck and she was pulling him down towards her.

Their mouths clashed, teeth scraped and bit. Clothes were torn, nails scraped down his back. They collapsed to the floor, too caught up in their passions to make it to the bed. Her fingernails bit into his buttocks and something savage in him broke free. His hands found her centre and he thrust his fingers inside her, revelling in her desperate moan as she jerked up to meet him. And then he was sinking into the heat of her. No thought of making it comfortable for either of them, his arms were braced above her, his knees digging into the hard floor as he thrust into her hard and fast. Her teeth sunk into his shoulder and he moved faster still. He sucked in a nipple and bit down. She cried out, pulling at his hair.

This was no gentle lovemaking; this was a fierce coupling. He wanted to brand her, to show her that she was his now and forever.

He alternated between licking and biting, pounding into her as she writhed beneath him. The angle was delicious, but it was not enough. He pulled out of her and flipped her onto her knees. She moaned as he sank back into her. From this angle, his hands could roam all over her. One began stroking her back, her thighs, her breasts, the other found the curls between her legs, playing with her there until she was crying out his name and pulsing around him. His own release was a blinding white light that rushed through him, stealing his breath and robbing him of his strength.

Hugh collapsed onto his back, pulling Bronwen with him so that she did not end up lying on the cold flagstones. Their harsh breathing filled the chamber, but neither of them spoke, the words of their argument lying between them.

Perhaps it was the anger that simmered between them or maybe the desperate need to feel something other than fury, but it was mere moments before he was hardening again. His hands roamed all over her, delving between her legs, over her buttocks, her thighs and over her breasts until she was writhing against him. And then she was pushing his hands away, and although it pained him, he stopped, because she may be his wife, she may belong to him in every way, but he would never force himself on her. She always had to be willing for his touch.

But he had misunderstood her intentions. Instead of moving away from him, she pinned his hands above his head before lowering herself onto his length. He could have pulled out of her grip, but the thrill of being at her mercy was too much. He held himself still as she rode him, using him to draw out her own pleasure. Her movements became jerky, and he knew she was reaching the end. His own release was building, heading towards something so intensely perfect he knew he would never be the same after it was over. They came together, an ending so blissfully powerful he was aware of nothing else.

She slumped down on him, her head resting on his chest, her hair splayed across his face, her legs on either side of his body. He slid his arms around her and held her close. Normally, they would speak after lovemaking, but neither of them said a word.

At some point, he must have fallen asleep, because when he woke, she was gone.

Chapter Twenty-Four

Bronwen shifted in her seat. Her body was wonderfully achy this morning. After she and Hugh had ravished each other—there really was no other word to describe it—she had made her way to the kitchens and found something to eat.

She had stayed away from the hall, knowing she would not be able to hide how she felt about her father's cronies now that she knew how much they were using him for their own ends. She had promised Hugh she would tell no one what he had discovered, and she would keep that vow. It was no use being upset with him for not being straight with her and then betraying her own pledge. Still, she was not going to be able to sit there and pretend nothing was wrong. She was not like Hugh, she thought bitterly, she could not hide her thoughts so easily. Those men would know she knew something as soon as they caught sight of her, and then Hugh's hard work and sacrifice would be for nothing. So she'd kept away, knowing everyone would assume she and Hugh were still enjoying their alone time together instead of wondering where she was.

She returned to her chamber much later, hoping her husband was still asleep. She could tell from the rigid way he held himself that he was awake, although he kept his back turned to her. She climbed into bed and lay down so that her back was facing him too. Tears pricked the backs of her eyes, but she would not cry again. She had promised herself that and she would stick to it. The night passed slowly. She slept in fits and starts, waking every time her body brushed his. She would move to the edge of the mattress only to fall sleep and find she had drifted back towards him. It seemed her body still craved him even though she had promised herself that her mind was back in charge of her actions.

As the sun streamed into the chamber, she awoke to find herself in his arms, his mouth seeking hers. They said nothing as their bodies began to move in the sleepy morning rhythm she so adored. They continued to say nothing once it was over, and he held her against him, the smell of his skin so deliciously familiar even after only three days together.

They said nothing as they climbed from the bed and readied themselves for the day, and they said nothing still when she let herself out and climbed the stairs to her mother's suite of rooms.

She and her mother had been working on her trousseau, and they were putting the finishing touches to it now that Bronwen had a name for her husband. There were embroidered blankets and sheets for her to take with her, although she had no idea where they were going to go because Hugh still had not told her where he was planning for them to stay.

'Mama,' she said when they had been working for a while.

'Yes, dear.'

'Would you like to come with me when I go to my new home? Hugh has said there will be a place for you, wherever it may be.'

Her mother's fingers continued to fly over the seam she was working on. She took so long to reply, Bronwen began to think she hadn't heard her. 'That is a very generous offer,' her mother said eventually. Bronwen had to hand it to Hugh, it was a lovely thing to suggest. There was a moment's waver in her anger and sadness before it flooded back. That Hugh was a good man was never in doubt; it was that their marriage was founded on a lie that was the problem.

'And? Will you take him up on it?' Bronwen pressed. She had seen her mother browbeaten by her father for long enough. This was a chance for her to move away from him. Her mother should be leaping for joy at the opportunity, but she seemed as docile as she always did.

'You are newly wed. You do not want your mother with you. Besides, I am married to your father and cannot leave him.'

It struck Bronwen then that she and her mother had never discussed the way her father behaved. They had merely watched from the sides as he had spiralled ever further into this mess they now saw before them. Bronwen had watched her mother slowly become destroyed by the actions, but they had never discussed them. Now might be her only chance. 'My father does not act as a husband should. He treats you terribly, he never has a kind word to say to you, and all the words he does say are cruel and degrading. You cannot surely want to continue living like this.'

Her mother peered at her over the edge of her sewing. 'I made a vow, Bronwen, to stay by your father's side in sickness and in health. I take that oath very seriously.' Bronwen had never heard her mother so solemn and sure of herself, and it struck something inside of her.

In the excitement of being married to Hugh and then the subsequent betrayal, it somehow had not properly occurred to her that they would be bound together for the rest of their lives. Was it really in her best interest to stay so angry with him? Living with it festering within her would cause her pain. It was just, right now, she could not get past the knowledge that while she was reluctantly falling for him, he had a hidden mission, one that had the power to destroy her and her mother.

'I hope that you will honour your wedding vows in the same way.' Her mother's tone was light but firm at the same time.

Bronwen had promised to stay with her husband, and she would keep that vow. They would be bound together for the rest of their lives, but she would not be like her mother. She would not give Hugh the power to hurt her. He would have no control over her heart, and therefore anything he said to her would not wound her, not any more. She had been in danger of falling for the man completely, but fortunately she had found out his true self before it was too late. She could guard herself going forward. 'I do not wish to be as unhappy as you.'

Her mother reached over and lightly touched the back of her hand. 'Nobody knows what goes on in a marriage aside from the two people who are in it. Your father and I may not be going through a good period, but there have been many times when he has made me happy. He has given me your brothers and you, which are gifts more precious than gold. Besides,' her mother laughed, 'I have seen the way Sir Hugh looks at you. I am sure you will not be like your father and me. Your marriage will be a successful one.'

Bronwen bit her lips together and focused her gaze on the point where her mother's hand touched hers. She could not tell her mother that her marriage had already disintegrated only three days after it had begun. They had not even had the time to go through a good period before the bad had started.

'Are you well, my love?' Her mother's question might have been her undoing. She may have cried and revealed just how hurt she was and why had a knock at the door not sounded at that very moment.

'Bronwen, you can tell me anything, you know.' Her mother tightened her grip on Bronwen's hands.

The knock sounded again. 'You had best answer that, Mama.'

Her mother sighed softly, but when the knock sounded again she straightened and called out, 'Enter.'

The door opened to reveal Hugh, his sharp gaze homing in on her straight away, and her stomach twisted oddly as she met his eyes.

'I am sorry to have disturbed you ladies,' he said, his deep voice sonorous and powerful, 'but I was wondering if I may have a word with my wife.'

'Of course,' said her mother, rising from her seat.

'I have been meaning to take a visit to the kitchen garden this morning. I will do so now.'

Bronwen would have insisted that her mother need not leave, but all her words were stuck in her throat. How unfair it was that her husband still looked so put together and composed when she was falling apart?

The door closed behind her mother, and the chamber plunged into an icy silence.

Hugh strode around the comfortable room, his hands clasped together behind his back, the floorboards creaking underfoot. Finally, he stopped behind the chair on which her mother had been sitting. 'I have been thinking and you are right.'

She started in her seat; she had not been expecting that. If he noticed her sudden movement, he didn't comment. She held her tongue, waiting for more, knowing that her father would never be able to admit that anyone else's suggestion was the better one. It was more evidence that Hugh was the better man.

'Approaching your father and appealing to his vanity may be the best course of action.' Bronwen nodded, she really did believe this was the best way forward. If her father was handled correctly, he could be persuaded to turn against the men who had helped make her and her mother's lives a misery for so long. Hugh coming round to her way of thinking and agreeing to listen to her suggestion was good, so why did she still feel so wretched? 'You have had years of dealing with him. How would you suggest I approach this?'

'I would not say you were sent here to spy on him.' The irritated words were out before she could stop them.

Hugh's lips thinned. 'I was not spying on him.'

'Then what were you doing?'

He paced to the unlit fireplace. 'I was sent here to find out the truth.' She winced at his use of that word, but if he noticed her reaction, he didn't comment. 'The vast wealth seen on display here made no sense, and my superiors wanted to know the reasons behind it.'

Although she longed for the truth, Bronwen almost wished Hugh would stop telling her everything. With every word that he spoke, he showed her again and again that he had not come to Ceinwen Castle for the tournament and to win her hand in marriage. She knew that knowledge would help her harden her heart against Hugh, but in the moment, his words only hurt her more. She could dwell on it, or she could move the conversation forward. 'Why have you decided to trust my father today when you were so adamantly against the idea yesterday?'

Hugh drew a hand over his face, his eyes were tight and pained. 'I have been waiting for Leo to join me so that I may proceed with the next part of my plan, but with every day that passes, it is becoming too dangerous for me to hold on. I must act soon, or else the treasonous act may take place. If I do nothing to stop it happening, then I am as guilty as the men who commit the crime.'

Bronwen closed her eyes as yet more horrible truths washed over her. She had thought she and Hugh had been enjoying the first few days of married life together, but he had been merely using her to pass the time while he waited for the next stage of his mission. She inhaled deeply and let her breath out slowly.

She was sure Hugh had enjoyed their time together, there was no way to fake the way he had come apart in her arms, the idea that he had been waiting for Leo somehow tainted the memory. What was done was done, and there was nothing she could do to take back the last three days. She would proceed with her pride and dignity intact. She brushed her feelings aside as she considered his words. She knew her father, and she thought she knew the best way to play to his good side. She had managed with the tournament after all, and it didn't matter that it had only been by the skin of her teeth. She had to hope that she guided Hugh right. Hugh may have hurt her, but that didn't mean she would thwart his mission for revenge, especially when treason was involved.

'My father will finish his private mass soon. If you are to act, it should be then. Come, I will walk with you, and we can discuss the wording on the way.'

He hesitated and she held her breath, hoping for something, although she wasn't sure what. In the end, all he said was, 'Very well. Lead the way.'

She stood and led him through a door at the back of her mother's chamber. This was not a set of corridors she walked often, this was the private rooms of the lord and lady of the castle, and even she was not encouraged to walk among them, but she knew the way and knew that it was unlikely they would be disturbed on this route. 'You should turn this situation around so that it appears to be my father's idea.'

'Yes, I agree with that, but how am I to do so?'

'Show him what you have found. You can be as incredulous as he is. Work him up into a frenzy and then suggest he have the men arrested.'

'Are the guards at the castle capable of such a feat?'

'You must have a high opinion of your and Leo's abilities if you think the two of you will be better than a host of guards.' His silence said it all. 'Oh, you do think you are better.'

'You've seen me fight.'

'Your arrogance is quite breathtaking.' He was the best swordsman she had ever seen, but he did not need to know that.

'I have been holding back,' he said simply.

'I still think…' But her words were lost forever when they rounded the corner and met her father coming the other way.

'What are you two doing here?' he demanded; his tone not encouraging, and his deep frown even less so. But at least his eyes had not yet taken on the dull, flat look he had when he was well into his cups. He was sober, or at least as sober as they would ever find him these days. 'Well,' her father snapped. 'Answer me.'

Bronwen couldn't think of a single word to say. They hadn't had enough time to prepare. They needed more. She should…

'I'm so glad to have found you, Lord Geraint,' said Hugh, his eyes wide with an innocence that looked completely fake to Bronwen. 'I have discovered something awful, and you are the only man who can solve the situation. As soon as I found it out, I knew I had to come to you.' Hugh was laying it on so thick, his words were like some dreadful paste. Surely her father would see his words for the manipulation they were.

'What can I do for you, my son?' Or perhaps not. Her father was looking at Hugh like a benevolent patriarch, taken in by Hugh's honeyed words.

'I think it would be best if I show you. You are

an honourable man, and I know you will not want to think ill of anyone if you do not see the proof for yourself.'

Her father's chest inflated and Bronwen was filled with a begrudging pride towards her husband. He had played her father perfectly, as he had her. 'Show me immediately.'

'Yes, my Lord.' Hugh turned to lead the way and Bronwen rolled her eyes.

Hugh was playing the meek subservient exceptionally well. As they wended their way through the castle, Bronwen watched Hugh work at her father. She knew him now. She knew the situation and she could tell he was not telling the truth, but the compliments he was heaping on her father seemed to be working. Is that what Hugh had done with her? Had he blinded her to what was going on by flirting with her? Their time together before their marriage had seemed so genuine, and yet it could have been as much a lie as his praise of her father.

The storeroom Hugh showed them was a shock. Even knowing what she did, Bronwen was taken aback from the sheer scale of the weaponry and the amount of gold coins stored here.

Her father was silent as he moved around the space, looking at each overflowing barrel and chest. 'To whom does this belong?' he said in a tone Bronwen had never heard before.

Bronwen held her breath, this was the trickiest part of everything. Getting her father to believe his friends had betrayed him would not be easy; getting him to act rationally after he had heard the news would be harder still.

'I am afraid your good nature has been abused,' said Hugh with false meekness.

'I can see that,' her father snapped.

Bronwen took in a small breath, but Hugh subtly shook his head. She frowned but said nothing.

'Ioan ap Cadfael is the leader.'

Her father's fists clenched, becoming tighter still as Hugh listed the names of the men who had lived at the castle for years, enjoying life at her father's expense.

'How do you know this?' her father demanded when Hugh finally lapsed into silence.

'I overheard them discussing their plans for treason this morning.' Yet another lie falling from Hugh's lips.

'Treason!' Her father clutched at his chest.

Bronwen rushed to his side, fearing the news might stop his heart, but he pushed her away. Only she heard her husband's low growl as he caught her around the waist, his grip as hard as steel.

'I'm fine,' she murmured.

Hugh snarled but made no comment, his arm still wound tightly around her.

On the other side of the room, her father staggered to the wall still clutching his chest. She tried to go to him once more, but Hugh held her close. 'Let him be a moment,' he whispered into her hair. 'It is a hard blow for him to take.'

They waited, the sound of her father's harsh breathing filling the air. Bronwen stayed within the circle of Hugh's arm, knowing she should step away from him but somehow unable to do so. She was grateful for his support when her father leapt away from the wall, causing her to flinch backwards.

'They must all pay,' her father bellowed.

Bronwen sagged slightly; her father believed Hugh. The first stage of the battle was won.

'Indeed, they must,' Hugh agreed, continuing to play his part as subordinate underling to her father's mighty lordship. 'What would you have me do, my Lord?'

'Nobody betrays the great house of Ceinwen and gets away with it.' Bronwen did her very best not to sigh; her father was now the one who was laying it on a bit thick. Since when had they been a great house?

'I will have my vengeance,' her father continued. 'They will know my wrath.'

This was all very well and good, but it wasn't actually a plan.

'You are right, my Lord. They should indeed feel the pain of your righteous anger.' Bronwen twitched. Was anyone ever going to get anything done, or were they going to spout pointless platitudes towards each other? The men could return to this chamber at any moment and then where would they be. 'If I may suggest something, my Lord?' said Hugh when Bronwen was beginning to think nothing might happen.

'You may, son.'

'Ioan ap Cadfael and the men I mentioned rode out on a hunt this morning. Or at least, that's what they told everyone they were doing. As they are liars, we do not the truth of their errand.'

'The blackguards, those fiends…' Hugh waited as her father grew ever more inventive with his insults. Finally, he ran out of things to say and went silent.

'We could close the gates and keep them out,' suggested Hugh.

As a plan, it was simple but effective. Without access to everything in this chamber, what did the treasonous men have?

'I want blood,' growled her father.

Hugh nodded, but now Bronwen doubted Hugh really agreed with her father. He was a consummate liar and had fooled her as completely as her father.

The knowledge reawakened her ire. 'We are at war with them. If they try to get into the castle by other means, we can rain down hellfire on them.'

'Yes,' said her father. 'Yes. I like this plan. I will stand on the ramparts so that I can see their faces when they realise I have bested them.'

'Very good, my Lord.'

Her father swept from the room, his head held high, the very image of wounded indignation.

Hugh glanced down at Bronwen when they were left alone. Neither of them made a move to follow him, but Bronwen was unsure of what she wanted. She was torn between railing at Hugh and pulling him closer so that she could kiss him. In the end, she settled for neither. 'That was well done. You had him convinced of your story.'

'It is because it is the truth.'

'You believe in all those flattering words you told him, do you?'

He sighed softly. 'I know you are angry with me, but I am only trying to complete my mission to the best of my ability. This route will keep your family safe. I thought you would be pleased.'

'I am, and I am grateful for what you are doing.' She felt his body relax against hers and realised she still stood in his arms. 'But that does not mean I can forgive that you lied to me, that you used me.'

'Bronwen...'

She could hear the anguish in the sound of her name, but she was not ready to hear his excuses. She did not know if she ever would be.

'We had better go and see what my father is doing,' she said instead. 'Who knows what he will do if he is not supervised.'

Hugh dropped his hold, and she immediately missed the warmth of his grip. She wanted to grab hold of him and to ask him to hold her forever, but he was already striding out of the room after her father, hurrying to do the job he had been sent to do.

They discovered her father in the centre of the courtyard. The normal activity of the castle inhabitants was slowly coming to a halt as people stopped to watch what he was doing. When her father was certain he had their attention, he bellowed, 'Close the gates, we are under attack.'

For a long moment, everyone in the vicinity of the castle froze. Some turned their heads to the archway where the surrounding countryside was clearly visible and no invading army was in sight. Nobody moved to obey him.

'You heard your lord and master,' yelled Hugh. 'Close the gates. Guards, head to your posts.'

On hearing Hugh's command, the people snapped into action. She had to hand it to Hugh, he was good at pretending her father was in charge while it was him who called the shots. He was more deceptive than perhaps he realised.

The gate creaked and groaned as it was lowered. Soldiers poured onto the battlements, fires were lit to heat water, and the women and children were hurried into the keep, deep inside the castle walls.

'You should go and join them,' Hugh said, gesturing towards the women.

'I'm not going to cower away from seven weaponless men,' she retorted.

'They have weapons.'

'A few arrows to catch a stag will not be a match for the men assembled here.' She pointed up at the walls. Men were at every station now, with her father striding backwards and forwards among them, shouting overblown encouragements about prophecies and greatness.

'Very well, but you will stay back from the wall, and if I tell you to retreat into the keep, you will do so without argument.'

'Yes, I will.'

'Promise me.'

'I promise I will retreat to the keep, should it be necessary.'

'No.' His eyes gleamed with fire. 'You will retreat

to the keep if I tell you to. Whether you deem it necessary or not, is not the point.'

She stamped her foot and then frowned at herself for her childish behaviour. 'Fine. I promise to retreat to the keep if you tell me to. Are you happy now?'

He gazed at her for a long time. 'Not really,' he muttered, turning away before she could question him on what *that* meant.

The mood on the battlements was almost festive. Bronwen supposed nothing much of interest normally happened around here, but first there had been the tournament and now there was this. It was more action than they had seen in years, certainly more than she had seen in her lifetime.

Hugh leaned against the battlement wall, his sharp gaze roaming the countryside, every line of him tensed for movement. This is what he had trained for, what he had spent years honing his skills for, and Bronwen could see the latent power in his pose. He seemed satisfied that there was nothing to see on the horizon and turned to pick up a bow, plucking at the string.

'What are you doing?' she asked.

'Checking whether it's taut enough.'

'Is it?'

'Aye. These are some good quality weapons. It will be satisfying using it against the men who prepared them.' He flashed her a grin, and despite everything that had happened between them, she couldn't help but smile back. Those men had plagued her castle for years, drawing out her father's worst behaviours. Yes, it would be very satisfying indeed to see their weapons used against them.

The morning stretched on, and there was still no sign of the men returning from their hunt. Warm rolls were handed round to the waiting soldiers who showed no sign of boredom at the lack of action. Bronwen was content to watch her husband in motion. While her father paced the walls, muttering words of bluster, Hugh inspected weapons, spoke to groups of men words of encouragement here, instructions there. Before long, all the men were turning to him instead of their lord, and Bronwen could not blame them. Hugh was a natural leader and they knew it.

Their marriage might be based on a lie, but perhaps they could forge something not built on love but on mutual respect. She could live without tenderness, had been planning to do so anyway, so there was no need for her to experience this overwhelming sense of loss. Their relationship could be the one she had always planned for; she could control her feelings now that she knew she had to be on her guard.

The way Hugh was handling the situation was the side of him that had drawn Bronwen to him in the first place: his sureness, his competence and his strength. She would happily watch him stride about commanding people all day. Perhaps that was just as well, she thought wryly, as she was probably going to have to follow him into battle as other wives of soldiers did. She really had made a mess of her future, and all because she had desired one man above all others. All the promises she had made herself, and she had made exactly the same mistake as her mother. Marrying a man who called to her soul rather than one who did not move her, committing to someone who had no home for her to go to.

At least Hugh didn't seem overly fond of wine and ale and wasn't given to making grand meaningless statements. Perhaps her future wasn't quite as bleak as she had feared.

When the rolls had become a distant memory, a sentry yelled from the top of the watchtower, 'They are returning!'

'Blackguards,' roared her father, shaking his fist. 'I shall rain down vengeance upon their heads.' Nobody turned to look at him. Instead they focused on Hugh, who was watching the approaching men, his eyes narrowed to slits.

Bronwen stood and made her way to a vantage point, remembering her promise to stay well back. There was a grim satisfaction from watching the men laugh amongst themselves as they rode towards the castle, only to stop when they realised the drawbridge had been pulled up and that the gate was firmly closed.

At a signal given by Hugh, the soldiers moved towards the crenelations, pointing their arrows down at the men gathered below.

There was a harsh delight in watching men she had loathed for years, men who had come into her home and disrupted it for the worse, finally realise that something was not right in their comfortable existence.

It was Ioan ap Cadfael who noticed the extent of the arrows pointed at them first. His jaw slackened as he gazed upwards, the others following him as they took in the extent of the hostility from the place they had all lived for years.

'Lord Geraint,' called Ioan. 'Surely there has been some mistake.'

'Has there? Has there?' her father shrieked. 'Why, yes, I believe there has. For years, I have treated you all as brothers, and *that* was a terrible mistake. You have abused my hospitality and taken me for a fool. Well, no longer, I tell thee. You are hereby expelled from Ceinwen Castle. All of you and your kin are forbidden from ever setting foot within these walls forever more.'

Ioan ap Cadfael had the effrontery to look offended. 'What is the meaning of this? I have served you well, Lord Geraint.'

'Begone.' Her father waved his arms to demonstrate how far Ioan and the other men should go, but still they did not move.

An arrow, sure and true, flew through the air landing directly in front of Ioan's horse with a resounding thud. The horse reared backwards, almost unseating the rider. Bronwen did not have to look to know who had sent the arrow. Hugh had told her he was an excellent shot, and he had not lied, at least not about that.

'Did you not hear Lord Geraint?' called her husband, his voice clear and powerful. 'He has told you to leave and never return.'

'You have no—'

Another of Hugh's arrows sailed through the air landing to Ioan's left. His horse spooked and reared up but unfortunately did not throw its rider, who clung to the horse's mane with an iron grip.

'These are warning shots, Ioan ap Cadfael,' Hugh called when his horse was back under control. 'But make no mistake, the third one I shoot will be a direct hit to your chest. After that, I will take down the rest of you one by one. Nobody in this castle will tolerate traitors to the king.' Hugh's voice rang true, and all the other soldiers standing on the battlements cheered at his words.

Ioan must have finally realised that his former home was out for his blood, because he turned to the men surrounding him and said a few words. Whatever he said had the men turning and riding away quickly. Arrows followed them, released from men who had been waiting all day for a fight and who had been expecting more of a resistance. The arrows flew wide, but it reinforced the message that the men were not welcome, as did the jeering sent to their retreating backs.

Hugh kept his gaze on them until they were no longer visible. 'They'll be back,' he said to Bronwen over the cheering. 'The stash they have here is too valuable to abandon.'

'You will stay though, won't you?' she asked, suddenly unsure if he would or not. 'You will make sure that the inhabitants of the castle are safe.'

'I will stay until I am certain the situation is resolved, yes.'

She nodded. She would have to be content with that answer, although she still had no idea what her future looked like.

'I need you to come with me now.' Hugh reached out his hand and held hers, tugging her along with him.

It only took a moment for her to catch on to his

intent, and then they were both stumbling down the steps that led from the battlements. It was too far to reach their chamber, so Hugh pulled them into the alley where they had once shared a passionate kiss. He lifted her skirts as she pulled him free of his trousers, and then he was lifting her and plunging into her in one swift movement. She moaned as his movements slapped her against the stable wall. It was rough and it stung slightly and she loved it.

Chapter Twenty-Five

In the week following the defence of Ceinwen Castle, the air inside became almost celebratory. Ioan ap Cadfael and his men returned a few times, but they were sent off with arrows and threats, and it had now been several days since the last sighting of them. There was still no sign of Leo's imminent arrival, and Hugh was unsure what to do about that. At times, he thought about leaving to hunt for Leo, but he held back.

He couldn't leave yet; there was too much left for him to do at Ceinwen. There was dealing with his father-in-law, who'd taken a shine to him, sorting through everything that Ioan had left behind, and all of that, *all of it*, was a front to put off having to leave Bronwen. He couldn't, not yet.

Perhaps it was wrong of him, but he wanted Bronwen to make the first move to heal the rift that had opened up between them. He'd risked everything when he had stood up in front of the hall and read his poem, had put his mission on the line, had made himself vulnerable in a way he had never done before. He needed to know for sure whether she had married him because of *him* and not because he was the lesser of two evils, and her anger with him, while frustrating, suggested that she did care after all. She would surely not be so upset if she had no feelings for him at all.

He knew that he had hurt her, but she had to see that everything he had done, everything that had happened, had been because he was trying to do the right thing. He was not like her father, not like Ioan ap Cadfael or his band of men, or even like her mother. He would always treat her well, and he would not withdraw from her like both her parents had. If she would let him, he would be the most constant presence in her life, but it had to come from her. She had to acknowledge that they were meant to be, and with every day that passed, he was beginning to doubt that she ever would.

The quiet between them was becoming a living, breathing thing that tainted his waking hours. The nights, however, were a different story. In the darkness of their chamber, one of them would reach across the chasm that divided them during the day, and their bodies would join. Sometimes their coupling was full of fire and passion, their mutual frustration being pounded out in a way that satisfied them both. Other times they were soft and sleepy, their bodies moving to an ancient rhythm until they were both so exhausted they would sleep, and then repeating the whole process the next day. Hugh hadn't realised such a torture could exist, and yet it did, and somehow he was losing himself in the delicious pain of it all.

Hugh was counting through a barrel of coins, trying to reach a total to give him some idea of how much wealth was stored in the room deep in Ceinwen. He had come to an agreement with his father-in-law that most of the coins should be handed over to King Edward but that at least some of it would stay with Lord Geraint.

That had been his hardest fought battle, and it had taken all of his flattery skills to get the man to agree to hand over to King Edward what Lord Geraint clearly believed was rightfully his by virtue of it being in his castle. Hugh had had to fight a similar battle over the weapons, but not so fierce, as Lord Geraint was not as interested in weaponry as he was wealth.

Adding up the coins was proving harder to count than the task would suggest. It was because his mind kept wandering to Bronwen. He was becoming increasingly desperate to see her smile aimed at him once more. Their time in bed may well be spectacular, and it really was, but he missed the friendship they had been starting to develop, missed the sound of her soft laughter that he was sure she never shared with anyone else.

The sound of movement by the door had him looking up hopefully, but his heart dropped when he saw it was not his wife but one of Ceinwen Castle's guards. 'There are two men here to see you.'

He straightened. Could this finally be Leo and Tristan? His heart twisted. If they were here, it was time for him to leave, and he still had no idea if Bronwen would choose to come with him. He could make her, she was his wife and had sworn before God to obey him, but that was not the marriage he wanted. Hell, it was not the sort of relationship he wanted with anyone. If someone did not want to be with him, he would never force them, and if his heart hurt to the point of breaking at the thought of being without Bronwen for months, possibly years at a time, he would keep it to himself.

'Show the men in,' he said to the guard, still waiting for his response.

He resumed his counting; there was still much to do, and he could not afford to take a break, especially if his departure was imminent. It was a while later that he heard a set of heavy feet sounding on the flagstone corridor outside. A second pair, lighter than the first, were following. He frowned. He would know his friends anywhere, and that did not sound like them. Leo, yes, but not Tristan. Before he could dwell on what that meant, Leo was bursting through the door, his friendly smile such a welcome relief that Hugh threw his arms around him, hugging him tightly.

Leo laughed, slapping him on the back a few times before moving away. 'You're looking very much at home here,' he commented. He moved towards the rich tapestries on the wall. 'Is that meant to be a horse, and what's it doing…? Oh no…' Leo frowned, and Hugh found himself grinning for the first time in days. 'Is that even possible?'

'I don't want to spend time thinking about it.' His father-in-law had a very odd taste in decoration, and Hugh spent a lot of time resolutely not looking at the walls.

Hugh turned to the person who had come in after Leo. It was not Tristan but a small, slender man with a slightly feminine physique. 'This is Sir Rhys,' said Leo, a hint of something that sounded like pride in his voice. 'Rhys is a new friend of mine.'

Hugh stared at the stranger, who was studying the tapestries in the room and not looking at him. Hugh looked back at Leo, who was gazing at Rhys with a look of utter adoration. Leo had never seemed interested in women, so it didn't overly surprise Hugh that he had fallen for a man. He should have seen that coming. What did astonish Hugh was that, in bringing Rhys with him, Leo had deviated from the plan, the plan which had been largely Leo's idea. Perhaps his friend would not be too surprised to find out that Hugh had also done so, although in a bigger, more life-altering way.

And then Bronwen was standing in the doorway, and all the air in his lungs rushed out, and he couldn't breathe. When would she be less lovely to him? When would his heart get the message that could not forgive him? When would his body stop craving her touch?

'Lady Bronwen,' he said, stepping towards her, only to stop when her cool gaze held him still. He cleared his throat. 'May I introduce you to Sir Leopold?'

She nodded her head regally. 'I have heard much about you, Sir Leopold. My husband speaks of you very fondly.'

Leo raised his eyebrows. 'Husband?'

'Lady Bronwen and I married last week,' said Hugh. Not saying that the first two days had been the happiest of his entire life, only for him to be placed into a hell of his own making.

'I see,' said Leo, appearing far calmer than Hugh would have expected when the news was revealed.

'I will not disturb you,' said Bronwen. 'I only came to ask whether you are planning to depart soon.'

'Yes.' He waited for her to ask him to stay or to give some acknowledgement that his leaving was not everything that she desired or even to say that she would come with him.

'Very well,' she turned, and just as coolly as she had arrived, she left.

Silence descended on the room, as thick as a heavy blanket. Rhys cleared his throat. 'I think I will check in on the horses,' he said.

'Good idea,' murmured Leo. 'But be careful.'

Rhys only laughed as he sauntered away.

'How did you come to have a travelling companion?' asked Hugh.

'Oh, no, my friend,' said Leo, grinning, 'we are not going to talk about me. I want to know how you have acquired a wife in the weeks we have been parted.' Leo sounded as happy as he ever did, even though he must know that things had changed dramatically and that this must have an impact on the plan the three of them had been working on since they were children.

Hugh swallowed past a lump in his throat. Leo and Tristan had been beside him through so much, but now Hugh wasn't sure that he truly wanted to follow the plan they had all worked towards, not when it meant being separated from Bronwen.

'She is very beautiful,' said Leo. 'I can see how you fell in love so quickly.'

'I'm not in love,' Hugh said. It was important that he not succumb to that fate. It was bad enough that his wife no longer liked him, but if he was in love with her, this would be torture. He could want to be with her but not be in love with her, couldn't he?

'Ah, I see.' There was a beat of silence. 'No. I don't actually see at all.'

'I won the tournament and the prize was Lady Bronwen's hand in marriage.'

'Hmm...'

'What does "hmm" mean?'

'It means that if you hadn't wanted to win the tournament, you wouldn't have.'

'No, I...' He rubbed his hand down his face. There was no point debating this. He had won the tournament, he had got himself a wife, who now appeared to despise him, and they were stuck together until one of them died, which would probably be him because he was sure his heart was splintering into a thousand pieces right at this moment. A fitting way to die, perhaps. 'I completed my mission,' he told Leo. It was important his friend know Hugh had succeeded in everything he had set out to do, even if gaining a wife had not been part of the plan.

'Good.'

'It was not Lord Geraint but his right-hand man who was guilty of treason.'

'That's just as well, considering you've married into the family,' said Leo cheerfully.

'I still have some things I need to sort out here, but I should be able to join you—'

Leo snorted. 'You can't still be planning on continuing with the plan.'

'Whyever not?' Hugh may have not wanted a future of campaigning as much as Leo and Tristan, may have lain awake doubting it was the right path for him, but it was the path he had chosen and he would keep his word to his friends. Besides, his wife did not want him by her side, so what difference did it make where he was?

'Things have changed. Neither Tristan nor I would expect you to carry on as before. You have a wife who, admittedly, I only saw for a fleeting moment, but who did not look cut out for a life following a group of men from battlefield to battlefield.'

Hugh shook his head. 'I took a vow…'

'None of us took a vow, Hugh. We were young and had not yet set foot in the world. This time apart has shown us that life is not as clear cut as we planned.'

'What has happened to you, Leo? You are spouting words of nonsense.' He wasn't. This was the calmest Hugh had ever seen Leo, but he couldn't allow himself to hope, not even for a moment, that Leo might not feel betrayed if Hugh did not continue with their plan. That would mean he would have to contemplate a life with Bronwen, and if she rejected that a second time... 'Fine, we may not have taken a vow, but I have taken our plan seriously, and I am not going to change that because your priorities have changed.'

Leo paused for a moment. 'I think, my friend, that it is you who has changed. But I can see that you are not to be reasoned with, so fine. We will meet again in two months in Windsor, where we shall present ourselves to Sir Benedictus as planned. I am sure that as soon as he looks on us, he will realise what fine knights we are and enlist us to his cause straight away.'

'That sounds like an excellent plan,' said Hugh, sounding stiff to his own ears. What was happening to him? He had always been able to talk to Leo, to laugh with him about nothing. Why did his friend's smirk make Hugh want to punch him? There had never been violence between them before.

'I wish you good day then,' said Leo, his gaze once more sparkling with mischief.

'Do you not want to stay? You could rest for at least a night.'

'As much as I would like to watch you make a fool of yourself over your wife, I have tarried long enough in getting to Tristan and should be on my way.' Leo's smirk turned into a full grin. 'I wonder if the mess he has embroiled himself in is bigger and worse than yours.' Leo laughed at his own joke and left without saying anything else, leaving Hugh wishing he had something to throw at his friend's back.

Hugh's life was not a mess. If anything, it was better than ever. He had completed his mission successfully. He had proved that Lord Geraint was not acting against the king and had stopped a treasonous act from happening. He had married a wonderful woman who may already be with child. He had everything to be grateful for.

If he occasionally felt the overwhelming urge to drop to his knees in front of Bronwen and beg for her to forgive him, nobody had to know that. He did not require her forgiveness anyway. He had done nothing wrong.

Chapter Twenty-Six

Bronwen waited near the entrance to the keep. Hugh and Leo had not seen each other in a long time, and maybe they would spend ages talking in the ante-chamber, but she rather thought they wouldn't. Leo had the appearance of a man who wanted to be in constant motion, and Hugh was bogged down with sorting through the mess Ioan ap Cadfael had left. Surprisingly, her father was being helpful. Perhaps it was the shock of discovering how close he had come to being unwittingly involved in a treasonous plot, or perhaps it was because of Hugh's steady hand, but her father's behaviour had been better, not perfect but much improved, and without the constant stream of criticism pouring from his mouth, her mother was blossoming. Things were better at Ceinwen, and it was all because of Hugh. Bronwen wanted to offer to help him, but that would mean crossing the chasm that had opened up between them, and she hadn't yet figured out how to do it.

Leo's arrival had brought something Bronwen had been avoiding thinking about for days. Hugh might leave with him. She and Hugh had not discussed whether she would leave when he did. She'd assumed but…things were not good between her and her husband. They didn't talk. Not really. Not of anything important, like their future. If he left her here…she glanced at the walls of her father's castle. She'd once thought them a prison, but everything Hugh had done here had changed that. The work he'd put in to eradicate any traces of Ioan ap Cadfael and his men had altered the place completely.

She could stay here, she realised. She could live with her mother and could cope with the man her father had become since his cronies had left, but to be here without Hugh…her heart cracked and she knew right then that living without Hugh was not an option. For better or for worse, she belonged with him, because not only was he her husband; he was also the man who, despite everything she had told herself, she loved. Being parted from him would not be a life worth living.

She began to pace, her hands clasped in front of her, a silent prayer ghosting across her lips, begging for her not to be too late to make things right between them. Not that much later, Leo emerged from the castle; her husband was not with him.

Leo's eyes lit up when he caught sight of her, and his mouth split into a friendly smile, one she was not sure she deserved. 'Lady Bronwen,' he called across to her, 'I was hoping to see you.'

Unused to such open goodwill, Bronwen could only smile up at him.

'I am so pleased Hugh has married you.'

'You are?' She'd understood that it was Leo who was keen for him and his two friends to travel on campaign together. If anything, Leo should be irritated that Hugh now had a wife.

'Yes. Hugh has always needed a family to love, and he obviously adores you.'

Heat coated her skin. 'Oh, no, I don't think it's like that. I rather forced him into our union.'

Leo laughed, a big booming sound that came from deep within his chest. 'No one can force Hugh to do anything he doesn't want to. Once he's made his mind up to do something, he is almost immovable. If you are his wife, it's because that was what he wanted.'

This was what she wanted to hear, it made the hard case around her heart crack open just a tiny bit, but Leo did not know all of it, and when he did, perhaps he would change his opinion. 'There was a competition and the alternative to Hugh was a man prone to cruelty. Stepping in and marrying me was the noble thing to do and we both know what Hugh is like.'

Leo nodded solemnly, even though his eyes still sparked with amusement. 'Hugh is honourable.'

Somehow that was both good to hear and awful. Good because it reinforced her belief that she had married a good man, even if he had lied about his reasons for being at the castle at least she knew that this man did not mean he would turn into her father. Awful because he may have married her to save her from Gwilliam and not because he wanted to be married to her at all costs.

'I know we have only just met,' said Leo, 'and you will probably think me very rude, but I would like to know why *you* married *him*.'

Bronwen opened her mouth to say that he had seemed like the best alternative, but what came out was something completely different. 'Because I love him.'

She had loved him since the moment she had seen him, and that feeling had only grown with every moment she had spent with him since then. It was why his betrayal had hurt her so much. She had wanted him to be at Ceinwen Castle because he wanted her as a wife, which she knew was irrational because none of the men competing for her hand had known her before they had arrived. For all she had wanted to guard her heart, she had failed, and that was why she was now in so much pain.

Leo's smile widened yet further. 'Then that's all there is to it.'

Leo made to walk away from her, but she had more to say. 'You say he adores me, but I don't think he does, and I know that you cannot know for sure, and I know that…' She stopped. Her desperation was making her lose her mind and forget how to speak in proper sentences.

Leo continued to smile his wide grin. 'Hugh is a simple soul, for all his intelligence. I could see from the way he looks at you that he cares very deeply for you. He wants you to want him for himself and not because he is a good warrior, and not because he can provide you with something and certainly not because he can get you close to our friend Tristan. If you can love him wholly and truly, then he will adore you for the rest of your lives together.' Leo nodded to her then and walked away.

Bronwen had a thousand questions, all about Hugh, but she let Leo leave. There was, of course, someone else who could answer them.

Chapter Twenty-Seven

Hugh trudged up the stairs to the chamber he shared with his wife. He was going to leave Ceinwen Castle tomorrow to head to Windsor. He may arrive before Tristan and Leo, but he was sure he could make himself useful while he waited for their arrival. He could stay here, but his wife did not want him, so what was the use in prolonging this torture? He may as well go now.

Except…if he left this castle, he had no idea when he would see his wife again, and the thought was intolerable. He stopped, foot half raised. What if he didn't go to Windsor at all? His heart leapt at the thought of doing something outside of the carefully constructed plan, the plan he had begun to doubt really was for him. He always did what was expected; he followed rules and spent his whole life trying to do what was right. He'd grown up with Leo's dream to join the King's Knights, and he'd taken that on as his own ambition, but now that he had spent some time away from his friends, he hadn't thought about it much.

When he stopped to really think about it, now on this narrow spiral staircase, he realised that what he wanted more than anything was to be with his wife, to make her love him as much as he loved her. If that meant living here in Ceinwen Castle, then so be it. The last few days, sorting through the mess left by Ioan ap Cadfael, had interested him in a way he had not thought possible. It was endlessly fascinating to work out how a castle ran and what improvements could be made to make it more efficient. He could have a life like this and be content—no, content was not enough. If Bronwen was by his side, his life would be better than perfect.

Now all he had to do was to persuade her that he should stay in her life. He may not have been the best choice of husband, but he would spend his life making her glad that she had picked him.

He entered their shared chamber to find it in utter chaos. For a wild moment, he thought Ioan had returned and attacked the one person who mattered most to Hugh. His hand twitched towards the dagger he always wore at his belt, but then he caught sight of his wife amid the swathes of fabric which seemed to be covering every surface.

She caught his gaze and smiled a tremulous smile, and his heart soared. The rigid lines of anger were no longer gripping her shoulders, and he stepped towards her. Before he could ask what was behind the thawing in her expression, there was a knock on the door. A servant entered and placed a large chest at the foot of the bed. Bronwen spoke to him briefly while Hugh watched, the realisation of what he was seeing finally sinking in.

'You're packing.'

It wasn't a question but she took it as one. 'Yes.'

She picked an embroidered sheet and began to fold it. It was larger than her and she kept dropping the ends. He made his way over to her and caught one edge. Together they folded in silence before she placed the neat material into the trunk.

'You're coming with me.' Again, he didn't quite phrase it as a question, even though her answer was the most crucial point of his whole life. His hands, so steady in combat, were shaking as he waited for her to speak.

'Yes.'

His knees nearly went from under him, but still he kept going. 'Because you have to, as my wife.' He shook his head. It was time to stop with these half statements and ask her what he wanted to know. 'Are you coming with me because you feel that, as my wife, you have no other choice?'

The wait for her response seemed endless. 'I will come with you wherever you go,' she said eventually. 'Whether it is to the edge of a battlefield or on some other mission, I will be with you because I do not have a choice.'

The hope that had built at the beginning of her words, plummeted at her revelation. She may not think she had a choice, but she did. If making her forgive him required giving her freedom, then that is what he would do. It could not matter to him that separating from her would cause him unimaginable pain. He would not let her sacrifice herself.

'Bronwen, I want you with me, but not at the price of your own happiness. So long as you are my wife, you will always have a choice to decide your own destiny. You—'

He would have carried on making his point, but Bronwen flung her arms around his neck and buried her face against his chest. His arms came around her and he hugged her tightly. They had made love many times, sometimes angrily, sometimes tenderly, but this was different. She was holding on to him as if she never wanted to let him go, and that was fine by him. He would hold her for eternity if that was what she required.

He had no idea how long they stood there, but eventually she lifted her head and gazed up at him. 'You don't understand,' she said softly. 'When I say I do not have a choice, it is not because I believe you will force me to do something against my will. I mean that I haven't had a choice since the moment I stepped out of the forest. It was always going to be you who were my husband. I may have fought against it for a while because of some preconceived notion I had about what qualities my ideal husband should have, but I didn't try very hard. From the moment we met, there was only ever you.'

Tears pricked the back of his eyes, but he was too caught up in the moment to feel embarrassment at his weakness. His wife wanted him, the man who had never felt truly worthy, the man whose own family did not care for him. She knew all this, and she still wanted to be with him.

He brushed a strand of hair off her forehead. 'It was the same for me. I knew I should stay away from you because of why I was here, but no matter what I told myself, I could not do it. I would have done anything to make you my wife from the moment I saw you too.'

Pushing herself up onto tiptoes, she brushed his lips with her own.

Before he kissed her deeply, there were things he needed to say to her. 'Sometimes I wish I had done things differently. I wish I had not had to lie to you, but I will never be sorry about becoming your husband.'

She nodded slowly. 'I wish you had not had to lie to me either.' He winced, opening his mouth to respond but she carried on. 'But I know you to be an honourable man. Everything you have done has been trying to make things better for those around you. Your friends, Sir Wallace, my mother, me... You are a good man, Hugh, and I am proud to be your wife. I will follow you wherever you need to go. I want to be with you more than I have ever wanted anything else.'

'And if we stay here? Would you mind living with your father?'

Her eyes widened. 'You'd want to live at Ceinwen Castle? I thought you wanted to be a renowned warrior. Present treasonous plot excluded, it's not very exciting around here. Your name will not be spoken about by the bards if we never leave Ceinwen.'

He shook his head. 'I've been living with Leo and Tristan's dream to become an elite warrior for so long, I think I believed it was what I wanted for myself without giving thought as to whether that was true. These last few days have given me a taste of what it would be like to run a castle, and I think I have an aptitude for it.'

Her lips twitched. 'You have an aptitude for everything.'

A grin burst out of him. Since Bronwen had found out the truth about him, he had been existing in a half state, but now, listening to her gentle teasing, it was as if the sun were coming out after months of relentless drizzle.

'I love you,' he told her. Beneath his palms, her muscles relaxed, and he was glad he'd told her, even if she didn't return the sentiment yet. He would spend the rest of his life proving to her that he was worth loving in return.

'All this time, I have been guarding my heart against you,' she said. 'And it was a pointless endeavour. I have loved you since the moment I saw you, and I will love you until my heart stops beating.'

He kissed her because he couldn't not. Her fingers threaded through his hair, and all thoughts of his future vanished from his mind as his body took over, but as his hands drifted down the length of her back, she lifted her head. He growled in frustration, trying to claim her mouth again.

She laughed. 'No, stop. We cannot do anything with the state this chamber is in. Help me to put things in trunks, and then we can...' She raised her eyebrows.

He nipped at her neck. 'I thought we might not go anywhere.' He certainly wasn't going to travel if it meant he had to put things away before he got to lay with his wife.

She wriggled against him as his hand began to draw intricate patterns against her skin, something he knew she loved.

'We must travel to Windsor,' she said breathlessly.

He groaned. That seemed like unnecessary hard work, now that he thought he might like to stay exactly where he was.

'You need to see what you are giving up, to be sure you are making the right decision.'

'Where you are is the right decision,' he told her, finally lifting his head to look down at her. 'It doesn't matter where I go because you are my home.'

She looked up at him for a long time, not speaking. He was content to let her look. He knew his sincerity was written across his face, and he wanted her to be able to see it, to know that she was always his choice.

'You're right,' she said eventually. 'There is no need for us to decide this very moment. There are better things we could be doing.'

And as her mouth returned to his, he was pleased to note she didn't seem to have any intention of clearing the chamber either.

Epilogue

Croxton Castle,
seat of the de Veilleux family
Forty years later

Bronwen followed one of her younger grandsons along the narrow corridor. He was almost bouncing with excitement at what he would find behind the closed door ahead of them. She bit her lip to stop herself from laughing out loud as he barged into the antechamber, not bothering to knock. Niall was lucky he had such an indulgent grandsire.

She reached the doorway to see Niall fling himself against Hugh's legs, as if they had been parted for months rather than less than a morning while Hugh worked his way through the castle accounts.

'What have we here?' Hugh boomed. 'Surely it cannot be my favourite Niall in the world. He was only a baby last time I saw him, and this young fellow is almost a man.'

Niall giggled, the sound so pure Bronwen's heart expanded with love. 'I am the only Niall you know,' he corrected his grandsire, 'and I am still six. Are you ready to play now?'

The book of accounts was still open on the table, several letters spread out to the side of it, but Bronwen knew Hugh would not say no to a game with his grandchildren. Not one of their children or their many, many grandchildren had ever had a reason to doubt just how much Hugh adored them or how pleased he was to see them. He had never made the mistakes of his own father and allowed one of his children to believe they were unloved or unwanted. Sure enough, Hugh said, 'I should like to speak to your grandmother first, but yes, I shall be along shortly. Prepare to be soundly beaten.'

'Never,' cried Niall, running to the door. 'We shall defeat you.' He stopped in the doorway, turning round to face them with a deep frown marring his forehead. 'You're not going to be kissing, are you?'

'I cannot guarantee that there will be no kissing,' said Hugh gravely, his eyes twinkling.

'Urgh. I shall tell the others we will have plenty of time to practise then. I don't understand why you both like doing it so much.' He paused. 'Even though grandma is very lovely.' He wrinkled his nose in disgust and then ran.

When Bronwen could no longer hear his footsteps, she lightly closed the door. 'Kissing, huh?'

Hugh made his way over to her, pulling her gently into his arms. 'I can always be persuaded to do more.'

'And disappoint the hordes of children planning to defeat you in the epic battle they have been planning all morning, I don't think so.'

He laughed and tugged her over to the comfortable chairs he kept in the room for when she worked with him, which she did often. Hugh did not think to shield her from work that was often considered to be a man's remit, valuing her input. It kept her busy, although it was hard not to be with their ever-expanding family. 'Sit with me a moment then, so I may rest before my legs are attacked by a barrage of wooden swords.'

She sat on his lap, because it didn't matter how comfortable a chair was; it did not compare to being surrounded by her husband's warmth. 'Anything to report from this morning?' he asked when she was safely tucked against him.

'Morgain is expecting again.'

They didn't need words for Bronwen to know how Hugh was feeling. 'Leo will be pleased,' he murmured into her hair.

That Leo's oldest son and Hugh's youngest daughter had fallen in love was a source of great happiness for the two men, although they never said so in words, which amused Bronwen, who knew that no matter how large and fierce the two men looked, they were soft underneath.

'How many grandchildren will that be?' Hugh asked.

'Well, Johanna is also expecting another one, so that will be…no, I'm afraid it's too many to count.' She and Hugh hadn't planned to create a dynasty at Croxton, but the castle had unexpectedly passed into their ownership several years after their marriage after the deaths of Hugh's older brothers. Bronwen hadn't mourned the men who had made her husband's early years miserable.

Instead, she and Hugh had built a family full of happiness and laughter, each year bringing more children to love. Being the matriarch to such a huge family was more wonderful than Bronwen could ever have imagined, and it was all because of the man who held her in his arms. Because of him and the way he had taken care of her over the long years of their marriage, she was always surrounded by people she loved and who adored her in return. Her life was more perfect than she could ever have imagined.

'Now, before you go outside to be conquered, I was promised some kisses.'

'Indeed you were,' agreed Hugh, who was only too happy to comply.

* * * * *

MILLS & BOON ®

Coming next month

ONE WALTZ WITH THE VISCOUNT
Laura Martin

Sarah made the mistake of looking up and for a long moment she was lost in Lord Routledge's eyes. Of course she'd noticed them before—even in the semi-darkness it was impossible to ignore the man's good looks. His eyes were a wonderful deep brown, full of sadness and intrigue.

She swallowed, her pulse racing and heat rising through her body.

She knew she was passably attractive, and there had been offers from a couple of young men of her acquaintance to step out over the last couple of years. Never had she been tempted. But, right now, if Lord Routledge asked her to run away into the night with him, she would find it hard to refuse.

Silently she scoffed at the idea. As if the poised and eligible Lord Routledge would ask her that. No matter what he said, he probably had five or six elegant and well-bred young women waiting for him downstairs.

'You look sad,' he said, an expression of genuine curiosity on his face. 'The waltz isn't meant to be a melancholy experience. At least not if I'm doing it right.'

With a press of his fingers he spun her quickly, and somehow they ended up closer than they had begun, her body brushing against his. She inhaled sharply, and for a moment it felt as though time had stopped. Their eyes met. Ever so slowly, he raised a hand to her face, tucking a stray strand of hair behind her ear.

In that instant Sarah wanted to be kissed. She felt her lips part slightly, her breathing become shallow. She'd never been kissed before, but instinctively her body swayed towards Lord Routledge. Her heart thumped within her chest as he moved a fraction of an inch towards her, and then stopped.

Continue reading

ONE WALTZ WITH THE VISCOUNT
Laura Martin

Available next month
millsandboon.co.uk

COMING SOON!

We really hope you enjoyed reading this book.
If you're looking for more romance
be sure to head to the shops when
new books are available on

Thursday 19th December

MILLS & BOON